A
Cat Burglar
Christmas

ALSO BY PAMELA GOSSIAUX

Mrs. Chartwell and the Cat Burglar (A Russo Romantic Mystery: Book 1)

Trusting the Cat Burglar (A Russo Romantic Mystery: Book 2)

Romancing the Cat Burglar (A Russo Romantic Mystery: Book 3)

Good Enough

Why Is There a Lemon in My Fruit Salad? How to Stay Sweet When Life Turns Sour

A Kid at Heart: Becoming a Child of Our Heavenly Father

Six Steps to Successful Publication: Your Guide to Getting Published

Ordinary Girl

Praise for Mrs. Chartwell and the Cat Burglar

An Amazon #1 Bestseller!

A New York Book Festival Runner-Up!

"Mrs. Chartwell and the Cat Burglar is a highly suspenseful, self-described romantic mystery that tugs at your heart and satisfies your intellect.

— John J. Kelly, *Detroit Free Press*

"Mrs. Chartwell and the Cat Burglar is a lovely story and I highly recommend it! It has everything you could wish for: mystery, suspense, romance and a great adventure. I just couldn't put it down!"

— Susan Keefe, *Midwest Book Review*

"Pamela Gossiaux is fast becoming a major player in the realm of writing. She deserves the wards and attention that are bound to come her way!"

— Grady Harp, *Top 100 Amazon* Hall of Fame Reviewer

"The story is well thought out, well written and well worth your time to read."
— William D. Curnutt, *Amazon Vine Voice*

"What a fun read! If you like the feel of movies on TMC you'll like this book. It's a good story spun with great lines and interesting characters."
— Diana Lesire Brandmeyer,
award-winning Christian author

"It's a cozy, uplifting read for anyone looking for a good story to curl up with. Optional accessories: a cup of something warm and a cat in their lap."
— Xanthe Muller, *Goodreads Reviewer*

"This is a mystery, perhaps a Cozy, but really much more, and is marked by constant cliff hangers and a great ending (that I won't give away)."
— Greg Jolley, author of the *Danser* novels

A

Cat Burglar Christmas

pamela gossiaux

Tri-Cat Publishing

Visit the author's website at: www.PamelaGossiaux.com

First Printing, November 2019
Library of Congress Control Number: 2019915563

ISBN 978-0-9987669-6-6 (paperback)
ISBN 978-0-9987669-9-7 (ebook)

Cover Design: Llewellen Designs
Formatting: Dallas Hodge, Everything But The Book
Author Photo: Vera Davis Photography
Christmas vector created by freepik - www.freepik.com

Published in the United States by Tri-Cat Publishing
Chelsea, MI

Tri-Cat Publishing

My Christmas Eve Angel
By Walter Hall
Circa 1948-1949

Long ago on Christmas Eve,
The first there ever was,
An angelic host announced a birth,
Sent down from Love above.

Decades later, but not too long,
An angel came again,
Announced a stone had rolled away,
Set us free from all our sin.

Time rolled on, as it always does,
2000 years and more.
Another Christmas Eve was come,
And my Angel, she was born.

The snow fell quietly that night,
So soft like Angel's curls.
The host rejoiced again on high,
A birth to change my world.

Every Christmas Eve was spent,
Celebrating Angel's life.
I never knew until I grew
That you would be my wife.

I saw you in a shop one night,
Filled with holly and evergreen
You bought those gloves, your cheeks
were bright.
Your smile, the brightest I've ever
seen.

I knew that night that Love had
sent me,
An Angel from above.
To have and hold on this cold earth,
Until we were called Home.

Death tried to take the babe on,
That first Christmas Eve.
But it failed and now He lives,
To save you and me.

Death tried to take my Angel on
A Christmas Eve ago.
An angel took her up instead.
She lives again, I know.

Angels watching over me.
Every day I've prayed.
My Angel watches over me,
We'll meet again, you'll see.

Long ago on Christmas Eve
The first there ever was,
An angelic host announced a birth
Sent down from Love above.

Chapter One

The snow fell quietly outside the windows of the old Victorian home. Inside, Tony was humming along with "O Holy Night" on the radio and hanging lights on the tree. His wife, Abigail, was in the kitchen making hot chocolate, the delicious smell wafting in to the living room.

"Smells yummy," he said to the small tortoiseshell cat that twined around his feet and batted at the cord. "Did she name you after her favorite drink?"

"I did," Abigail said, coming into the living room. She set his mug on the coffee table, because at the moment he was tangled in lights. She took a sip of hers. "I got her on a cold day. I was sitting on the couch petting her, and sipping my cup of cocoa and thought the name fit her perfectly." She reached down to stroke her cat. "And it does. She's warm and sweet."

"That she is," Tony said. "Just like you. Cocoa, maybe I can get Mommy under the mistletoe later, huh?"

The cat meowed.

"See? She'd like that," Tony said, setting the last of the strand on the tree and then reaching down to plug the lights in. A soft white glow filled in the branches. "All done."

"It's beautiful," Abigail said. She came up behind him to look at the tree, and wrapped her free arm around his waist. He could smell his wife's lavender shampoo on her long, red hair.

"So are you," he said, turning and kissing her. They were still newlyweds, not even married a year. He doubted he'd ever get tired of holding her close, even after *fifty* years. "Do you want me to show you how much I love you?" He raised an eyebrow and gave her his most charming smile.

She laughed. Not quite the reaction he was hoping for.

"Let's finish the tree first," she said, reaching over to pick up a small white ornament. It was a pair of porcelain angel wings. "This one used to belong to my grandma." She hung it just above one of the small lights on the tree. "Grandma loved angels."

Tony looked at it, and it reminded him of his favorite movie, *It's a Wonderful Life.* He still couldn't believe *this* was *his* life. It *was* a wonderful life, just like the movie. When he met Abigail, he had been a thief, making a living taking from others. And then somehow, God decided that Tony was worthy of more and brought Abigail into his life. Tony had worked hard to change, in order to be with her, and didn't regret it. He couldn't imagine life without this woman.

"O Holy Night" ended and a new Christmas carol came on.

"Oh, I *love* this one!" Abigail said, her eyes bright.

"Me too!" Tony said. A romantic at heart, this Christmas song had always been his favorite. "My Christmas Eve Angel" was a classic, and one of the most popular Christmas songs of all time.

"I have the book!" Abigail said suddenly, and set her mug down on the coffee table. "I'll be right back!" She ran upstairs.

"The book?" Tony yelled after her. "I didn't know there was a book!"

He started to sing quietly along with the song.

Time rolled on, as it always does,
2000 years and more.
Another Christmas Eve was come,
And my Angel, she was born.

"Here!" Abigail said, coming back downstairs with a children's picture book in her hand. "My parents gave it to me one year at Christmas. I think I was maybe six years old. Come and sit with me on the couch." She patted the spot next to her. Quickly, Cocoa jumped up and took Tony's place.

"She still isn't used to sharing," he said, picking Cocoa up and sitting down. He put the cat on his lap. She bristled a moment, her tail twitching, then decided to settle down on his lap. She began to wash her paws.

Abigail opened the book. The watercolors were beautiful, depicting a nighttime scene from the very first Christmas Eve in Bethlehem. Mary and Joseph were in a stable, and Mary was very pregnant, her hand on her belly.

By now the song was over on the radio and a new Christmas pop song that Tony wasn't familiar with was playing. He tuned it out as Abigail stared to read.

"Long ago on Christmas Eve
The first there ever was
An angelic host announced a birth
Sent down from Love above."

Tony reached for his hot chocolate and took a sip. The book was well read, the edges of the pages worn. The pictures in the book were beautiful, and depicted a host of angels singing.

Abigail continued,

Decades later, but not too long,
An angel came again.
Announced a stone had rolled away,
Set us free from all our sin.

"My grandma loves this song," Tony said, running his fingers over the written lyrics on the page. "I bet she had no idea there was book, or we would have owned it." His grandma raised him after his parents died, and his deep love of books came from her. It was no wonder he had married a librarian.

Time rolled on, as it always does,
2000 years and more.
Another Christmas Eve was come,
And my Angel, she was born.

Abigail stopped and looked up. "It's such a sad song," she said. "Such a sad story."

"Not really," Tony countered. "I mean, they lived a good life. Together. And now they are together again."

Walter Hall wrote the song in the late 1940s. Tony had watched a documentary last Christmas on the songwriter. A candy maker of modest means, Walter penned only a few songs in his life, all of them Christmas songs, but none had become popular except for "My Christmas Eve Angel." His wife Angela, his "Angel," had died of pneumonia, on her birthday, which was Christmas Eve, a year before the song had come out. The documentary said that Walter, who had fallen asleep in a chair by his wife's hospital bed, woke to see an angel walk into the room and take his sick wife's hand, and he knew then that she was in Heaven. The song—and the story—had grown in popularity over the years and was the most popular Christmas song in America, second only to Bing Crosby's "White Christmas".

Tony listened as Abigail read about Angela's birth, and how Walter met her one night while Christmas shopping. He had stopped in a store to buy his sister a pair of gloves, and there she was. Angela. His true love.

"You're *my* angel," Tony whispered when Abigail quit reading to turn a page.

She turned to look at him beside her on the couch, her lips dangerously close to his. "And you're mine," she said softly. He wanted to kiss her, but she turned back to the book. She read through the rest of it to the end. When Walter's Angel left him, Tony tried not to think about what would happen if Abigail died. His jolly mood of earlier turned a little bit sad.

Abigail turned to the copyright page. "1962," she said. "But I think the song was written much earlier."

"The late 1940s, I believe."

She sighed. "So long ago." She closed the book, and they sat there quietly.

Tony could hear Cocoa purring, and feel the vibrations on his lap. The cat was peacefully asleep. He thought about how safe he felt when he was with Abigail, in her arms at night, or even just here next to her on their worn couch, a hand-me-down from her aunt. Then he thought about the close calls they had over the past several months, and how he had almost lost her to the hands of a dangerous man. And how she had lost her first husband in a car accident.

"Do you think we have angels watching over us?" he asked.

Abigail reached over to stroke Cocoa on the head. The cat stretched out her front paws luxuriously. "Of course we do. Otherwise I wouldn't have *you*," she said. She raised her eyes to meet his. "Our angels have kept us safe. God has kept us safe."

"But what if He doesn't?" Tony asked. "Or what if our angels are busy doing other things when we really need them?"

"I don't think it works like that," Abigail said. Her faith had always been stronger than his. He still sometimes wondered where God had been when his mother died of cancer, and his dad left him and died a few years later in a ditch, consumed by alcoholism.

"I think we have angels watching over us, and that our angels are empowered by our prayers," Abigail said.

"So…the more I pray the stronger my angels are?"

"Maybe."

Tony thought about that. He knew that Abigail and his grandma both prayed for him every day. He decided to go with that. "I guess I'm pretty well covered then," he said.

"That you are," Abigail said. She turned to face him. Her lips were close to his again.

"So like Walter, I have both guardian angels, and my own angel," he said to her.

"Yep."

She smelled amazing. He leaned in for the kiss. But she pulled back and raised an eyebrow.

"I'm waiting."

"For what?" But he knew.

She simply smiled, so he tried to think of some Shakespeare. It was their thing, how they met. He had quoted a romantic line from Shakespeare and won her heart. Or at least it had been the *start* of winning her over.

"An angel; or, if not, An earthly paragon," he quoted, trying to make his voice sexy.

"That's the best you can do?" she teased.

"Woman, I'm distracted!" he said, and moved in again for the kiss. But she turned her head, and he got a face full of hair.

"An earthly paragon?" she quoted, bringing her finger to her chin in thought. She turned back to him and her eyes narrowed. "Hmmm. I'm thinking. A paragon….a paragon of what? Virtue?"

Tony grinned. "Not if I can help it."

Abigail giggled. He was finally going to get that kiss when Abigail's phone rang. It was beside her on the couch and the loud noise made her jump. Cocoa, startled, bolted off Tony's lap, digging a few claws in his thigh.

"Ouch," he said.

"You okay?"

"Maybe."

Her phone was still ringing.

"I'll just ignore the phone," Abigail said, and her lips met his. They were soft and welcoming. Tony tried to ignore the sting where Cocoa's claws had dug through his jeans. The phone quit ringing, and then immediately started up again.

"I should check it," Abigail whispered. Her hair was tickling his nose.

"Yep," he said, and leaned back on the couch. Maybe he should go put some peroxide on his leg.

"It's Naomi from the church," Abigail said, looking at her caller ID. "I wonder what she wants."

She answered it.

"Abigail!" Tony could hear the woman's excited voice coming over the phone. "This is Naomi. We were just decorating the tree for our Christmas Eve service and you'll never guess what we found!"

Abigail looked at Tony. "I'm putting you on speaker," she said and clicked it over.

"Is Tony there too?" Naomi asked. She was the church administrator, an elderly woman around age eighty.

"It's me, Naomi," Tony said. He couldn't help but smile. Naomi had really taken to him when he started attending the church.

"Oh Tony, you handsome devil, you," Naomi said.

Tony met Abigail's eyes and grinned.

Abigail shook her head in mock disbelief. "What did you find?" Abigail asked.

"Oh, it's too exciting!" Naomi said. "Maybe it's a fake. But I don't think so. That's why we need you, and your expertise."

"What is it?" Abigail asked again.

"You should come and see. You *have* to come and see. It'll be a surprise."

Abigail looked at Tony. "Okay. But we're tied up in something right now. Maybe tomorrow?"

"No! It can't wait," Naomi said firmly. Tony had never known her to be excitable, so this was out of character for her. He had to admit, now he was *really* curious.

"Come *now*," Naomi said. "You won't regret it. I promise!"

When Abigail hung up the phone, Tony eyed the mistletoe that hung near the entry to the kitchen. "Later," he said, grinning.

"I promise," Abigail said, and gave him a quick kiss on the cheek. "Let's go."

Chapter Two

The small protestant church sat on a corner near the outskirts of campus, but it was just close enough to the university that a solid number of their attendees were students. It was an older building, erected in 1902, and built of brown brick. There were no stained glass windows, but instead its main attraction was a big bell tower that tolled hymns every day at noon, spreading the praise of God across campus.

It was nearly 8 p.m. and dark outside. Tony parked the car at the curb and Abigail climbed out, pulling the hood of her coat over her head against the light snow that was falling. Tony came around, took her hand, and together they walked up the recently salted steps. Evergreen decorated with red bows draped the large wooden doors. Each door held a big pine wreath garnished with matching red bows.

"Pretty," Abigail said.

"Mmmmm," Tony replied, and pulled one of the heavy doors open for her to enter.

"Abigail!" Naomi's voice echoed up the long aisleway and across the narthex. Abigail saw her up at the front of the church, standing on a small step ladder. "I see a bare spot up here so I….just… need…"

Abigail cringed as Naomi stretched her body, reaching up above her head with the shiny gold bulb. The step ladder teetered a little bit.

"Let me get that," Tony said, letting go of Abigail's hand and jogging up the aisleway.

Naomi turned and smiled, dropping her arm. "Thank you, Tony," she said, as he offered her a hand down. He took the bulb from her.

"Where do you want it?"

"Right there," Naomi pointed. Tony was tall enough he didn't need the step ladder. Abigail pulled her hood down off her head, shaking the snow off. Naomi was already hustling over to the choir pews, where she carefully lifted a box and brought it to Abigail. "Wait until you see this."

Naomi set the box down on the floor and kneeled beside it. Abigail and Tony peered down as she rifled through some paper. "Come!" Naomi motioned for them to kneel as well. Abigail pulled her boots off and she and Tony did as beckoned.

Naomi was unwrapping an ornament. It was an angel, dressed in a white linen cloth that had yellowed with age. The angel had golden hair and a golden halo painted on its head. As Naomi lifted it up, the head fell off.

Abigail and Tony both gasped.

"No. No, it's okay," Naomi said. "It's not worth anything. And thank goodness. Randall, with his big hands, bless his heart. He dropped her this evening. But look what we found." She reached her fingers down inside and pulled out a piece of paper. Carefully, almost reverently, she unfolded the paper. The sheet was about four inches by six inches, unruled and thick. Almost like drawing paper. It too, was yellowed with age, like the angel's clothes.

"Careful," Abigail couldn't help but say. Working with old documents and maps was her specialty at the university library, and she always got nervous when amateurs handled antique items.

Naomi was careful. She opened it, and they scooted together to read from the lights above the pulpit.

My dearest Angel,

I am writing you a song. You bring music to my heart, and I rejoice every morning that you are by my side. I'm afraid I'm not good at speaking the words you need to hear, so I have to write them.

I saw you in a shop one night,
Filled with holly and evergreen
You bought those gloves, your cheeks were bright.
Your smile, the brightest I've ever seen.

I knew that night that Love had sent me,
An Angel from above.
To have and hold on this cold earth,
Until we were called Home.

You are my all, my everything,
My light, my breath, my treasure.
Promise me you'll never leave
I'd be lost beyond all measure.

Angel, my life began the day you entered it. Let's be together, always.

Love,
Walt

Abigail felt a tingling in her stomach, the excitement she always got when she found an old map or book. Exploring a document like this was like being transported to the past. Especially when it was hand-written, like this one was.

But even more exciting was who she suspected the author was.

"Walt…." She whispered. "Walter Hall."

"That's what I think!" Naomi said excitedly and too loudly, and waved the paper a little bit. Her hands were shaking.

"May I?" Abigail asked, reaching for the letter to keep it safe.

"Of course. You must!" Naomi said. "Can you figure out if this is authentic?"

Abigail took the paper in her hands. The feel of it was twentieth century, she could tell by the fibers. The writing looked like fountain pen, which put it before the mid-1950s.

"Are there any other documents to match the handwriting to?" Naomi asked.

"I'm sure there are," Abigail said. "It's certainly the right timeframe to be him."

"This is amazing!" Tony said. "We just heard his song tonight, and then Abigail was reading the book to me when you called. Then again, I guess that song is played all the time during the holidays, so maybe it was just coincidence."

"I'll take it to work tomorrow morning and check it out," Abigail said. "This is *so cool!* He's my favorite Christmas singer, and my parents used to read me the story of his song every year at Christmas."

"This letter was to his Angela," Naomi said.

"Yes," said Abigail. "I wonder why he left it in this angel?"

"Maybe it was a Christmas gift to her," Tony said. "An angel for his Angel."

They sat there in silence, the three of them, looking at the letter Abigail was holding. She read it silently again, letting the ramifications sink in. If this was indeed a letter from Walter… and especially a love letter to Angela, it would be worth a lot to a collector. She almost didn't want to share it, to flaunt his private love for the world to see.

"Look," Tony pointed carefully. "Those are some stanzas from the song."

"I wonder…" Abigail said. "I wonder if he started writing a song for her, and then she died before he finished it? So the song changed."

"Well," Naomi said. "That's what we need for *you* to find out." She started to stand. "These old knees!"

Tony effortlessly stood and offered her a hand. He gently pulled Naomi up. Abigail carefully refolded the letter, tucking it back inside the angel. She set it in the box, closed the flaps, and stood.

"Where did you get this?" she asked.

"We found it in the donation box," Naomi said. "Our own angel tree topper was a bit decrepit with age and Randall found this one, so we thought we'd use it. It's a bit cheap and too small for our tree, but it's all we had. And then he broke it, and we found this inside."

Abigail smiled. "I'm pretty sure this is authentic. I can't wait to research it tomorrow. This may be the best Christmas present I get this year!"

"I could give you a better one," Tony said under his breath, his voice suggestive. She gently elbowed him.

"I heard that," Naomi said. "I may be old, but I'm not deaf. Behave yourselves in church." Then she chuckled. "But when you get home, that's another story!"

Abigail felt her cheeks redden. Her fair complexion was a curse. She saw Tony's eyes on her, crinkling with humor. She reached up and ruffled his wavy, black hair. His Italian good looks caught the eye of most women, even eighty-year old ones.

"Who dropped it off?" Tony asked. "If Abigail figures out what it's worth, who gets to keep the letter? Or the church could sell it and use the money for missions or something, right?"

Another thing Abigail loved about Tony was his sense of compassion. He was always trying to figure out ways to help others.

"I think it would be more beneficial to the previous owners of this angel," said Naomi.

"Trisha Borgnine dropped off this box a few days ago. She's a single mom and is cleaning out her house to make a room for the youngest. She wants to move him out of her room and into his own, and has made a nice little bedroom in the attic. Which is I guess where this was stored."

"Trisha Borgnine," Tony repeated. He vaguely knew her from seeing her around church. She had a few kids. "Where does she live? We can stop by and ask more questions about it."

"Over near the south side. They ride the bus to church. I'll have to look up her address."

Abigail expected to follow her to the church office, but instead Naomi pulled an iPhone out of her jeans pocket and started tapping on it.

"Here. It's in the church directory," she said. "I can barely read this."

Tony took her phone. "Here it is," he said. Abigail felt her phone buzz as Tony shared the contact with her. "Naomi, there's a way to make your text bigger so it's easier to see," he said.

As Tony started to fix Naomi's phone for her, Abigail pulled her boots on and slowly walked down the aisle, carrying the box. Tony, a techy, was in his element, and would be a while. She walked to the back door and sat down in a folding chair, the box on her lap.

If this was really Walter's letter to Angela, Trisha Borgnine's world would change forever.

"Let's go there now," Abigail said excitedly, when they were back in the car.

"*Now?* Where?" Tony asked.

"To the library. I want to do a bit of research on this. It's not even 9 p.m. I can't wait until morning."

He drove her to the big university library where she worked, and she let them in with her set of keys. She loved the library at night. Always quiet anyway, nighttime left it a sanctuary of silence, a great place to think, rest, or clear one's mind. She locked up a few nights a week, the last to leave, and those work evenings were always her favorite. Surrounded by old maps and documents, books, stories from the past, she felt shrouded in a world so different from her own.

And at this time of year it was even more beautiful, with a full-sized Christmas tree in the atrium.

Abigail went past the front desk and into the maps and ancient documents area on the second floor. She switched on the light at her desk, then went into the workroom at the back, turning on the lights there. She washed her hands at the sink and carefully dried them.

She pulled an archival-safe sleeve from under her workstation, and set it on the desk where Tony had placed the box.

"Ready?" She asked her husband.

"Always." Tony loved old things too.

Some of the documents that Abigail worked with regularly were very old, ancient, and from hundreds of years ago. This one was only from the last century, but it might be difficult to pinpoint a date. Wood fibers, pulping chemistry, paper additives and surface treatments could all serve as dating markers through a qualitative analysis. But she didn't really need that here.

Abigail carefully opened the box and lifted out the angel. Then she pulled the letter out and unfolded it. "We know the approximate date," she said, turning on her desk lamp and swinging the magnifier around.

She studied it for a few moments.

"You're sexy when you work," Tony said quietly into her ear.

"Stop it. I'm concentrating."

"So am I."

Abigail smiled, and turned to look at him. "It's definitely written with a fountain pen," Abigail said, "and not a ballpoint, which dates it pre-1956."

"Ballpoint pens were a thing of the 50s?"

"That's when they would have been affordable. Before that they cost around $10, which would be roughly about $100 today. Walter was a man of modest means, and a candy maker by trade, so he would never have paid that much for a pen."

"Angela died when?" Tony said, pulling out his phone and opening Google. "According to Wikipedia, she died in 1948."

"And we know she was still alive when he wrote this letter."

"I wonder…" Tony said. He turned the angel over and looked underneath it. There was a company name stamped on the bottom. Tony typed more into his phone. "Look. This company produced these angels *only* in 1948. They didn't sell well, so they discontinued them the following year." He turned it over and looked at the cherubic face and painted-on halo. "No wonder," he muttered. "So if they were only made that year, and she died that year..."

"Then he bought it for her just before she died. Maybe that's why he wasn't able to give it to her."

They both stood there looking at the angel silently. Finally, Tony said, "That's so sad."

"It is."

Abigail had faced the loss of her own spouse seven years back, when Nick was killed in a car accident on an icy winter night. She had almost lost Tony this past year when he was shot on their honeymoon in Paris. Reflexively she grabbed his hand, entwining her fingers in his.

"Don't ever die, Tony Russo. Not without me." Her voice came out as a whisper, and suddenly she felt very afraid.

"That's not my promise to make," Tony said. "But I can promise that I will do my best not to."

They both knew there were no guarantees in life. They had found that out personally.

Tony squeezed her hand. "I have my guardian angels watching over me. You and Grandma keep me going with your prayers. I'm a blessed man."

Then he let go of her hand, and in true Tony style, lightened the subject. He picked up the little plastic angel again. "I sure wouldn't want *this* angel protecting me," he said.

Abigail looked at the sweet cherub cheeks. "It's cute."

"C. S. Lewis has a quote about that," Tony said. "Let's see…" This one he had to look up on his phone. "He says 'In scripture, the visitation of an angel is always alarming; it has to begin by saying 'fear not." The Victorian angel looks as if it were going to say "there, there."

Abigail laughed. "True enough!"

She looked at her watch. "I have to get to bed. I'm due back here at 7 a.m. tomorrow."

"Ouch. Yes, let's go home."

"I'll talk to my appraiser tomorrow, and see if he'll analyze the handwriting to confirm it's Walter's. I'm pretty sure there are other documents out there we can use to compare with. Walter is a famous man."

She carefully slid the letter into the archival-safe sleeve, and locked it in her drawer. Then she put her arm around her husband. "Let's go home."

Chapter Three

The next afternoon was cold and snowy, and Tony was glad for the new gloves he had purchased last week. A sharp wind blew from the north, bringing the temperatures into the teens. It was in no way a perfect day to be scaling up the side of a building on the north side of town. But because it was dark from the clouds, and because the jewelers were all out to lunch, it made it the perfect time to break in. Plus, the blowing snow made for good cover.

So Tony steadily climbed the rope, thinking how he should have worn white instead of his black spandex suit. Daytime was not his motive operandum for breaking into a building. Nighttime was clearly the better alternative. But married life had forced him into a schedule and he had to be home by five to make dinner.

He stopped at the second floor window, because he saw movement. Hanging to the side, he used a mirror to peek in. A woman was getting water from a water cooler. He stayed out of sight and pulled himself higher up on the rope, until he reached the third-story window. People often didn't alarm windows up past the second floor.

They didn't think anybody would be able to get into them.

They thought wrong.

Tony peeked in the window, but he knew from research that nobody would be on this floor at this time of day. This was the room where the jewelers worked, forming gold and silver into place settings for precious stones. The items were sold down below, on the first floor, in the shop. But the action—and the loose stones—were all up here.

The floor appeared to be empty.

Pulling out his phone, he ran it along the perimeter of the window, using an app that detected electrical activity. Just as he suspected, no alarms were installed. A gust of wind blew him sideways, and he nearly dropped his phone, but the grip on his gloves helped him hold on to it. He silently thanked the Gods of glove-making. These gloves, which he had recently purchased, were phenomenal. They kept his hands warm and were light enough so he could work. He glanced down at the ground. More than thirty feet below him, a hard, icy sidewalk beckoned and he understood why the jewelers didn't think anyone would be stupid enough to climb this building.

But they didn't count on *him*. He had to pay the bills somehow.

Slipping his phone into his pocket, he clipped the rope to his harness so his hands were free. Then he pulled a tool from his bag, which Abigail referred to as a baby toilet plunger, and suctioned it to the window. Using a glass cutter, he carefully cut a circle around it, pulled the piece of glass out, slipped his hand through, and unlocked the window. He opened it, climbed inside, and looked at his watch.

Under five minutes to get inside. He was *that good.*

Tony looked around. The tables had been cleaned up and the stones put away. He looked up at the cameras. The cat burglar suit he was wearing hid him well, but that didn't matter. He had disarmed the cameras from his laptop in the warmth of his car just a few minutes ago.

He scanned the room. Someone had put little Christmas window clings up and there was garland sagging along the far wall.

There. A picture on that same wall that hung slightly crooked. He walked over to it, pushed it aside, and found the safe. He pulled out a stethoscope. It only took him an additional minute to get into the safe.

Inside were several drawers lined in black velvet. He pulled one out. Amethyst, rubies, emeralds. He pushed it back in, and pulled out the second. This one held what he was seeking— *diamonds*, cut into a variety of shapes and sizes. He fingered the largest one, briefly calculating what it would sell for on the black market. Tony was very familiar with stones and their value, from his years of stealing. He left it and picked out two of the moderately expensive ones, slipped them into a velvet pouch he was carrying, and closed the safe. It would take them some time to discover that they were gone, which would give any thief time to sell them on the black market, or be out of the country.

And their combined value of just under $500,000 would buy a nice plane ticket.

Tony reset the combination, put the picture back in place, and climbed back out the window. When he closed it, he replaced the piece of glass with a new epoxy he had. He pulled the shade down just enough to hide it until the epoxy dried clear.

He was quickly down the rope and back in his car. The whole process had taken less than twelve minutes.

He was pulling off his mask when someone rapped on his driver-side window. He jumped. It was a cop. One he didn't know. A new guy. Probably a rookie. He rolled down his window.

"Sir, what are you doing?" the police officer said. His hand was resting on the gun at his hip.

Tony swallowed and resisted the urge to run. "I'm working. This isn't what it looks like."

"I need to see your driver's license."

If he ended up in jail, Abigail was going to kill him.

"I've got a friend at the police station. Can we call him?"

"He's with me!" A voice boomed through the wind and snow. Tony saw with relief that it was the owner of the shop, Joseph Weber. The cop approached the owner and the two huddled in conversation. Weber produced a few items from his wallet, and the cop shook his head. He came back to the car.

"Looks like it's your lucky day," he said, and left.

Weber came around and opened the passenger door and climbed in. He shut it and Tony rolled the window up against the cold wind.

"You weren't able to get in!" Weber said triumphantly.

"I *was*," Tony said, grinning, and produced the two diamonds from the bag. They sparkled in the light against the black cloth of his glove.

Weber stared in disbelief for a moment, then looked at Tony. "Well, I'll be..." he said. "How'd you do it?"

"You really need to tighten things up around here," Tony said, and he began to explain the shortcomings of Weber's security system.

Back home, Tony pulled off his cat suit and climbed into the warm shower. He was freezing. His job as the owner of Black Cat Security got him into some pretty challenging situations. He had to admit he enjoyed it more in the summer. But it paid well. Nowadays he was showing business owners how to keep people out of their buildings and protect their wares. It was kind of the reverse of what he used to do. But he liked it.

After he had showered, dried and dressed, he made himself a sandwich. Cocoa twined herself around his legs, begging for a scrap of lunchmeat.

"It's roast beef," Tony told her. "Not in your natural diet."

She meowed louder.

"Really. I can't see you taking down a cow." But he pulled off a piece and gave it to her. She ate it and looked up for more.

"That's all," he said, and sat down at the table. His phone rang. It was Abigail.

"My appraiser's not in today, so I'll have to go tomorrow," Abigail said. "But he told me to see if I can trace where the angel and letter came from. What city. That sort of thing. Why don't you go over and check out that family, and see if you can find out more?"

"Sure thing," Tony said. "I had planned on doing that after lunch. I need a break from the Weber case."

"How did it go this morning? Did you get the job?"

"Yep. I proved to him he needed me. And almost got arrested doing so."

"I'm not surprised."

Tony could imagine Abigail rolling her eyes. He smiled. "Love you," he said.

"I love you too. See you tonight."

After she hung up, Tony pulled on his jacket and found the scrap of paper Naomi had written their address on. He took it and headed over to the Borgnine household.

It was a ten-minute drive away, on the other side of the river. As he crossed over the bridge, he noticed that the river was frozen. The nights had been so cold that even the rushing waters had lost their battle to the temperatures. Still, he would never chance going out on it. Rivers never froze completely.

The housing district on the south side was made of smaller cookie-cutter homes, built cheaply for the flux of southerners who came north looking for work after WWII. This particular neighborhood was run down. Some houses had windows boarded up, and those that were doing better had cheap, gaudy Christmas decorations on their lawn.

When he came to 426 Irvine Street, there were no Christmas decorations. There wasn't any landscaping either. Just some brown, dead weeds sticking up out of the frozen snow drifts against the house. Tony pulled into the driveway, and shut off his car.

The front door was open, despite the cold, and a dog barked at him through the frosty glass of the storm door.

He went up and knocked. From inside, over the barking dog, he could hear a baby crying. When nobody came, he rang the doorbell. That's when a thin, blonde-haired boy appeared. He was barefoot, wearing jeans that were too short for him, and a striped t-shirt. He narrowed his blue eyes at Tony.

"Who are you?" he said through the glass.

"My name is Tony. I go to your church. Is your mom at home?"

"Benny! Shut the dog up!" the woman yelled from somewhere in the house. Benny pushed the dog back away from the door and said something to it. It quieted down. It was a chocolate lab mix, and once Benny had talked to it, it started wagging its entire body in Tony's direction. He decided it wasn't much of a threat.

"Mom! It's some guy from our church!" Benny yelled into the house. Then he looked at Tony again. "I know you!" he said, and his eyes lit up.

A young woman came towards the door, the screaming baby on her hip. Her short, dark curly hair was a mess. She smiled at Tony and opened the door a crack.

"Hi, Tony. I vaguely recognize you. I'm sorry—we aren't in church much."

"No worries," Tony said. "I just have a quick question about the donations you brought in last week. Can I come in?"

She hesitated, but only for a moment, then opened the door. "I'm afraid it's a mess in here."

Tony went in, carefully stepping over a pile of books on the floor.

"Benny, why is this front door open? It's freezing outside," she scolded, as she pushed it shut. She turned to Tony and offered her free hand. "I'm Trisha."

"Nice to meet you," he said. He vaguely recognized her too.

"Mom! This is that thief from church who found that famous painting!"

He glanced at Benny, who was dancing a little bit in his excitement. He figured he'd get right to the point.

"You donated a box of Christmas decorations last week," Tony said.

"That's right," Trisha said. "I need to clear out some space for Henry here." She motioned to the baby on her hip. He had stopped crying and was staring at Tony. Henry was dressed in a pilled navy blue sleeper with footies. There were spaceships on it. He looked to be about a year old.

"Hi, Henry," Tony said, giving him a little wave.

"And this here is Benny," Trisha said.

"Mom! Do you remember him?" Benny said. "He's famous!"

"But yes, that old box of ornaments," Trisha said, ignoring her older son. "Those used to be my momma's. When I married Darren, she gave us some to start our own tree."

"Dad isn't coming home for Christmas this year," Benny said. The light in his eyes died.

"Mom!" Another voice called from a room Tony couldn't see. "I spilled the milk!"

Trisha sighed. "I'm coming!" She trudged into the kitchen, and Tony followed her. The linoleum floor was peeling. Faded wallpaper, striped with chickens on it, lined the walls. It wasn't pretty. A small, scruffy girl of the same coloring as Benny was holding a dripping half-gallon carton of milk. Most of it was on the floor at her feet.

"Oh, Marla!" Trisha moaned.

"I got it," Tony said, taking the paper towel roll and bending down to sop up the milk.

"I'm so sorry!" Trisha said. "It's a mess. I'm going to be late for work."

She put Henry in a high chair, and knelt down with Tony, helping him wipe up the milk.

"I'll get it," Tony said. "You go get ready for work."

"Thanks." Trisha didn't argue. She had dark circles under her eyes, and looked like she hadn't slept in a week. Or maybe months. She hurried out of the room.

"Dad isn't coming home for Christmas this year," Benny repeated.

"No?" Tony looked up at the boy, whose arms were crossed tightly against his chest. If it was possible for a ten-year old to look angry at the world, then that was Benny.

"Nope. And I say good riddance."

"Hmmm." Tony stood and looked at Marla. She looked like she was about six years old. "Where's the trash?"

She opened the cabinet door under the sink, and Tony threw the soaking paper towels into the trash.

Then he turned to Benny. "Why?" he asked.

"Why what?" Benny put his hands on his hips.

"Why isn't your dad coming to Christmas?"

"Because he's going to his girlfriend's instead," Benny said. "Mom says good riddance."

"I see. And how do *you* feel about that?"

"I say good riddance too."

Tony felt he should get to the subject. "Where did your mom get those Christmas decorations?"

"They were my grandma's, before she died."

"Where did Grandma live?"

Benny shrugged. "Somewhere we used to drive to in the car."

This wasn't much help.

Suddenly Trisha hurried into the room, putting an earring in her ear lobe. "I've got to get to work," she said to Tony. "Why is it that you stopped by?"

"I was trying to track down where the angel ornament came from," he said.

Trisha was looking in her purse, counting coins.

"Um…I don't know. What angel ornament?"

"There was a tree topper in the box you donated. An angel."

"Maybe…" She seemed frustrated.

"You're busy. Now isn't a good time," Tony said.

"Benny? I need a dollar," Trisha said. "Do you have one in your piggy bank?"

"Moooom!" he moaned. "That's *my* money!"

"I need it for the bus."

"But it's my—"

Trisha turned and gave Benny a firm glare, the same type Tony's grandma had used on him from time to time.

Benny sighed, slumped his shoulders, and disappeared.

"I have a dollar," Tony said, pulling out his wallet.

"No, that's okay."

"Better yet, why don't I give you a ride? I'm on my way back into town. Where do you work?"

"Shakey's Pub," she said.

Tony knew where it was. Just on this side of the bridge. "That's right on my way home." Plus, it would give him time to talk to her.

She hesitated. Benny came back in the room and grudgingly held up the dollar.

"She doesn't need it," Tony said. "I'm going to give your mom a ride to work."

Benny's eye lit up. "Yes!" he said, pumping his fist into the air and then pushing the dollar into his pocket.

Trisha looked at Tony. "It's not necessary."

"Yes, it is. It's silly for you to take the bus when it's on my way."

Trisha nodded and bent down to give Benny a hug. "Bedtime is at 10 p.m. Henry will need a bottle." She turned to follow Tony out the door.

"You're leaving them alone?" he asked.

"The neighbor girl will be over shortly," she said.

And sure enough, a girl who didn't look much older than Benny showed up at the door as they were walking out. She wasn't wearing a coat, and was chewing on a wad of gum.

"Thanks Tanya. I've got to run!" Trisha said as the girl came inside.

Tony followed Trisha out to the car, glancing back at the door. Benny stood there with the dog next to him, waving, until they backed out of the driveway. Then he closed the door, and Tony wondered what the rest of the evening held for those kids.

Chapter Four

Abigail was alone at the library, except for Bob, the night janitor, who was downstairs mopping. It was her day to close, and she was sitting at her desk soaking in the silence since her coworkers had left a few minutes ago.

She stacked up the maps brochures on her desk, and a few accidently slid off onto the floor. As she reached down to pick them up, she remembered the night she met Tony. It was a cold night like this, not quite a year ago. She had been tidying up her desk before leaving, and he had slipped down through the skylight above, from a rope, dressed in his black spandex cat burglar suit. He thought the place was empty, and was as surprised as she was when she stood back up from the floor and they saw each other.

Her first reaction had been fear, but then Tony had said something to put her at ease immediately. Which, thinking back on it, was just *weird*. She should have screamed.

But Tony had pulled off his mask, quoted a romantic Shakespeare line, and she had immediately fallen in love with his dark eyes with their thick lashes, and how they sparkled with mirth.

He had won her heart immediately, and she had stalled in calling the police. And then helped him escape when they arrived.

Now, much later, she wore his ring on her wedding finger. He had given up the life of crime for her, and she had never been more in love.

She needed to get home to him, and the warm dinner she knew he would have waiting.

Abigail pulled on her coat, shouted a goodnight to Bob, (even though he probably couldn't hear her with his earbuds in) and let herself out the front door. It was snowing, and even though there wasn't any wind tonight it was bitterly cold.

There were fourteen steps down to the sidewalk, and sitting about midway down them, under one of the lights, was a person. He (or she?) was wrapped in a dark coat, and swaying slight from side to side.

Probably one of their homeless. They came to the library in the winter and often sat inside to warm themselves up. Ms. Scott, the library director, frowned on it, but Abigail often turned a blind eye, or pretended they were doing research if she saw them.

She felt a pang of sadness, but walked down the steps and towards her car, not intending to engage the person in conversation.

"Miss?" She heard him call from behind her when she reached the bottom step, but she chose to ignore him, and turned towards the parking lot and away from the voice.

"Miss!" he shouted louder. She felt she had no choice but to acknowledge him. It would be rude not to. While the university campus was usually safe, one could never be too sure, so she avoided strangers. But it was early, only 7 p.m., and there were others around, walking back from classes or on their way to get dinner.

"Can I help you?"

He motioned for her to come closer. She walked back up the steps towards him, and stood a few feet away, out of arm's length.

"I'm cold," he said.

His grey coat was thin and covered with snow. He wore a toboggan cap on his head, and was a white male who was maybe in his sixties. It was hard to tell. He had beard stubble, and smelled quite bad. She recognized him then as a man she had let sit in the library to get warm on a few occasions this week. His coat was different, but it was him. He had seemed harmless enough at the time. But you never knew. She thought of stalkers and how they lured their prey in by acting normal.

"Cold and hungry." He unfolded a hand from his coat and reached it out to her. His cotton gloves had holes in them.

"Um...." She started to rummage in her purse. Maybe she had a few dollars for him. He would probably spend it on booze.

But she had nothing.

"I'm sorry," she said. "I gave the last of my change to my co-worker today." Pauline had forgotten her lunch money.

"Please help me," he said.

"Isn't there a shelter you can go to?" she asked. She knew it sounded cold, but she didn't trust him.

He shook his head. Then she heard a tiny mew. From inside his coat he produced a small, grey kitten. It was skinny and pathetic looking. "I need some food for Lily too."

Abigail thought of the stereotype of white vans with puppies offering unsuspecting children a ride. But her heart started to melt.

"Where did you get Lily?" she asked. "I haven't seen her with you before. Have you had her in the library?"

He nodded, and touched the large grocery bag that sat next to him. "She usually stays in here. I've only had her a short while." He put her back inside his coat.

Abigail sighed. She looked up to Heaven, then at the library. She couldn't think of a place for them to go where they wouldn't be kicked out. The men's shelter wasn't too far from here, but she doubted they'd let pets in. Still, she'd try that.

"All right. Come on," she said. She reached over and took his bag. "I'll get you to the shelter."

He stood. "Thank you."

The only reason she was doing this was that she rode the bus today. She felt they would be safe in public.

"What's your name?" she asked him when they reached the bus stop.

"Mr. Bates," he said.

When the bus came, she let the driver swipe her card twice to pay for Mr. Bates ride. When they were seated, she did a phone search on the men's shelter. It was on Fourth Street. The bus didn't go that way. She'd have to get off at Pontiac, catch the 22nd, then take that to Fourth. This was starting to sound like a lot of work.

The man smelled terrible, and she tried not to gag. He probably hadn't had a shower in weeks. She looked at him, sitting across from her, and he smiled. Some of his teeth were missing.

The kitten stuck it's head out of his coat and started yowling. Cats weren't fans of riding in autos, and this one wasn't either.

The bus driver glanced back. "There are no pets allowed on the bus," he said. "You will need to get off."

Oh no.

"It's a therapy pet," Abigail said. "You know... one of those comfort animals."

"Does he have a license for it?"

She glanced at Mr. Bates. "Do you?" she asked, to kill time.

"A what?" he asked.

The kitten continued to yowl.

"Sir, you have to get off at the next stop," the bus driver said as he pulled up. He opened the door and frowned at them.

Now what? Abigail didn't feel right abandoning Mr. Bates and his kitten. They were pretty far from the homeless shelter, and this stop was more residential, so now Mr. Bates was further from the main streets of the city, where he could beg for help.

They got off together. She sighed, unsure what to do next.

The kitten popped it's head back inside the coat and quieted down.

This bus stop was five blocks from her house. In nice weather, she had gotten off here before and walked. Tonight wasn't nice, but she *was* wearing her boots. She would take him home and then she and Tony could drive him to the shelter together.

"Follow me," she said. She was probably going to get herself knifed. Tony would kill her if this man didn't.

But he ambled along quietly beside her.

"I appreciate this," he said. "I really do. I lost my job."

"It's okay," Abigail said. She was glad the streets were well lit.

Nothing more was said on the long walk back to her house. When she got there, she was relieved to see that Tony was home. His car was in the driveway. She pulled out her phone and texted him that she was outside with a guest.

Tony opened the door before they got up the front steps. His look of shock told her she should have warned him who the guest was.

But Tony always had good manners. "Hello sir," he said, smiling. Then he looked at Abigail, his eyebrows raised in question.

"This is Mr. Bates. He has no place to go tonight. I thought maybe we could drive him to the shelter?"

"Sure," Tony said. "Let me get my keys. I..um...I need to turn the oven off. Why don't you come in for a minute?"

He opened the door wider, and Mr. Bates and Abigail stepped inside. She saw Tony grimace at the smell, and her own stomach did a somersault. Lily poked her head out and meowed.

"And he has a cat," Abigail said.

"I see that," Tony said.

As Abigail stepped further inside, the smell of dinner overcame the smell of Mr. Bates. Tony had a roast chicken on the table, with mashed potatoes and a salad. Something was baking in the oven that smelled wonderfully like chocolate. He had outdone himself.

Mr. Bates was looking at the food as well. He was pretty round, so not starving, but looking malnourished nonetheless. His big belly could be from worms or the wrong kind of foods.

Tony saw him looking at the dinner. He glanced at Abigail.

"Are you hungry?" he asked the man.

Mr. Bates nodded.

"Maybe he could shower first?" Abigail said.

"I'll take you to our guest shower," Tony said. He took the kitten, and handed it to Abigail. "Follow me," Tony said.

Abigail held the kitten to her chest and heard it purring. She was a bit ashamed of her uneasiness towards Mr. Bates, and vowed she'd do better when he reappeared. She heard the water running, and a few minutes later Tony came into the kitchen.

"He's showering."

"I hear."

She was still standing there holding the kitten. Cocoa, who had come to greet her, was now standing over by the couch, her tail puffed. Occasionally she would hiss.

"I need a box," Abigail said.

Tony ran to the basement, and came up with a tall box that their new washing machine had been delivered in the other day. They put the kitten in it.

"I'll give her some food," Abigail said, taking her coat off. "Then I'll get us something to drink and keep the dinner warm. Why don't you keep an eye on Mr. Bates?"

"Got it."

About ten minutes later, Mr. Bates emerged a new man. Tony had given him some clean clothes—sweat pants and an old sweatshirt of his own.

Abigail took the aluminum foil off of the food that she had covered it with to keep it warm. "Have a seat," she said. "I fed your kitten and she's sleeping." She indicated the box where the kitten was. Lily had quieted down, curled up sleeping on an old towel that Abigail had provided.

"Thank you," Mr. Bates said. He sat down at the table and picked up a fork. "Smells good."

"We usually pray first," Tony said.

"Oh. Sorry." Mr. Bates put his fork down and bowed his head. Tony blessed the meal and then Abigail served their guest.

He didn't say much. Abigail tried to start conversation, asking him a few questions, like where he was from, but it was hard to pull information out of him. She learned that he was born in Idaho, then came to Michigan for a job, then had a few problems with alcohol, but he kept his answers short and vague.

She didn't smell any alcohol on him now.

"Where do you live now?" she asked.

He looked at her. "On the streets, currently," he said, "but I thought you had figured that out."

She looked at her plate and picked at her potatoes. She felt like she was badgering him, so she and Tony switched to talking about work. Soon, thankfully, dinner was over.

"There's a men's shelter down on Fourth. Tony and I will drive you there."

"They won't let pets in," he said.

"I'll take care of Lily," Abigail said. Tony gave her a look across the table, so she added, "for now."

It was after 9 pm. so the shelter was officially closed. But they rang the bell and a shelter worker came to the door. The man was tall and lanky with stringy hair. He told them in an unenthusiastic voice that the shelter was nearly full, but he could probably find a bed.

Abigail had bagged the dirty clothes and handed Mr. Bates that, along with the grocery bag the kitten had been in. He had a few belongings in there, including a book on cat care, a measuring tape, a spool of thread, and two pairs of socks.

"Thanks," he said. He looked at Tony. "Thank you for the clothes. And both of you for the meal."

"Mr. Bates, we'll get you some toiletries," the shelter worker said.

Mr. Bates shuffled inside and the worker closed the door, leaving Tony and Abigail standing on the steps, the snow falling quietly around them.

"I guess that's that," Tony said.

"I guess," Abigail said quietly. "Do you think we should have done more for him?"

"I don't know," Tony said. He took her hand. "Let's go home."

Abigail let Tony lead her back to the car. "Most of us are only a paycheck or two away from that," she said.

"I know," Tony said. "Believe me, I know."

On the drive home he told what he had learned from Trisha.

"The angel tree topper was her grandma's, and she's not sure where she got it. Grandma used to travel and loved Christmas, so she was always buying ornaments when she was out of town. She was also an avid peruser of garage sales, so bought Christmas stuff there. Trisha and I figured that's where she got it, since it wasn't new."

Abigail thought about that. If that was the case, they'd never be able to track down the original owners.

"Walter had obviously opened the box. But there's just no way to track where it came from," Tony said, confirming her thoughts. "Her grandma apparently had so many Christmas ornaments when she died that they gave most of them away. Trisha had just kept a few boxes, but this year she wasn't even able to put up a tree."

Tony told her about how exhausted Trisha had seemed. "And she was on her way to work a night shift after having worked her day job."

"It's so unfair that people have to live like that," Abigail said. "I can't even imagine trying to juggle three kids on top of a job, with no help."

"At least when *we* have kids, we'll be there to help each other."

"Promise?"

"Always."

She glanced over at him. She loved the way his hair curled, even when he tried to straighten it with the hair dryer. She longed to touch it. He was a gentle man, and she loved the tender way he treated her. He was great with the cat, and was always looking for ways to help the people in their lives.

"You'll make a great father," she said.

His smile spread from ear to ear. "You think?" He reached over and took her hand, giving it a little squeeze. "And if our daughters look anything like you, I'm going to have a hard time keeping the boys away from them!"

Abigail smiled.

Tony continued. "Trisha wouldn't say anything about her personal life, so I did a little digging when I got home."

Abigail gave him a sideways glance. She hoped he used legitimate means to search. She decided not to ask.

"Trisha is divorced as of last year. Her husband was a loser—lost his job at a factory and never picked up work after that. Won't pay child care, lost his driver's license, and is now missing. Presumably he ran. So Mom is left to pick up the mess, raise three kids on her own, and work two jobs."

Abigail sighed.

"I'll check with the appraiser tomorrow," she said. "If we can confirm that the letter is authentic, we can probably find a buyer. Sounds like she could use the money."

Tony nodded, and they drove the rest of the way home in contemplative silence.

Chapter Five

After Abigail left for work the next day, Tony got a call from a number he didn't recognize.

"Hello?"

"Hi Tony, this is Trisha Borgnine. You gave me your number last night and said if I needed anything…hold on."

She must have put her hand over the receiver because her voice sounded muffled. "Marla, I told you not to give the baby that. He'll choke! Tony?" Her voice was louder now. "You still there?"

"Yes."

"I'm sorry. I'm in a fix. The babysitter is refusing to watch Benny today because he put a spider in her shoe last night. Apparently when she put her foot in the shoe, it crawled up her leg. She says she'll watch the other two, but not him. I need to get to work and he's off of school for the holidays, and I have no place for him to go. Later today I'll have the second babysitter—the one you met last night. She'll watch him. But until then…"

Tony knew what she was asking. He had never kid-sat in his life. He wasn't sure he wanted to start now.

"Well…"

"You said if I ever needed anything. I am *so* sorry to ask. I have no one else at the moment. Naomi highly recommends you."

"Naomi?" Tony heard a loud wail in the background, which sounded like Henry.

"Marla!" Trisha's voice was muffled again. "Don't tease him! Give him the cookie!" Then, "Tony?"

"Um, sure. But he'll have to hang out with me while I meet a client. I have a lot of work to do today."

"Oh, I can't tell you how much I appreciate this!" she said. "You're a lifesaver! I don't need you until 9 a.m."

Tony told her he'd come and pick Benny up. Then he hung up the phone. What had he gotten himself into?

He looked at his watch and decided to leave now so he could drive past the shelter and check up on Mr. Bates. The snow had picked up and the temperatures were supposed to drop this evening. He wanted to make sure Mr. Bates had a place to stay tonight, and tell him that Abigail was taking care of his kitten.

He found parking along the curb of a street one block over. When he stepped out of his car, he saw a familiar-looking shape huddled on a bench across the street. The wind was whipping the man's scarf violently, and snow was piling up on his grey coat.

Tony crossed the street. "Mr. Bates?" he said.

The man lifted his face so Tony saw that it was indeed Mr. Bates. Tony sat down beside him. He wondered what he was doing out here, but it was hard to talk in this wind.

"You want some coffee?" Tony said.

Mr. Bates nodded. Tony got up and Mr. Bates followed him down the street to a little coffee shop. They went inside, and Tony ordered them each a coffee, and then as a second thought, he bought two sandwiches.

They sat down and Mr. Bates hungrily unwrapped his sandwich and started eating.

"Oops," he said, looking up. "You want to pray first?"

"Um, yes," Tony said. He said a quick blessing.

"So," Tony said. "Did you sleep well last night?"

Mr. Bates nodded. "Excellent," he said. "I was finally warm."

Tony smiled and took a sip of his coffee.

"You staying there again tonight?"

"Yep. I have my own bed." Mr. Bates took a sip of his coffee, then held it between his red hands to warm them. Tony wondered where his gloves were.

"Abigail is taking care of your kitten. She's going to take her to the vet today for a checkup."

"I miss Lily," Mr. Bates said.

"What is your first name, if I may ask?"

Mr. Bates shook his head. "It doesn't matter."

Then, because he didn't know what else to talk about, he told Mr. Bates about Benny and his family. He didn't mention their names because it felt like gossip. But he needed to unload.

"That little boy seemed so angry, and he's only ten," Tony said. "I guess you can't blame him. He needs a father." It had been bothering him a lot. He remembered how he was, when his mom died and his dad left him, drawn to alcoholism from his grief. If his grandmother hadn't taken Tony in, he had no idea how he would have turned out. Or where he would have gone. His grandma wasn't rich, but they always had enough money to live comfortably. And he went to a school in a decent part of town.

"The kid goes to a pretty rough school," Tony said. "The same school district I went to, but the building he's in is over on the other side of the bridge and has some pretty rough kids in it."

"Sounds like he needs a lifestyle change," said Mr. Bates.

Tony thought about the letter. He looked over at the man. "Do you believe in God?"

Mr. Bates shrugged. "Do you?"

"Yes." Although he struggled with why God didn't intervene more in the lives of His people. "Do you ever pray for Him to take you out of your current situation?"

"Into what?"

The question surprised Tony. "I don't know." He thought how to frame his answer without insulting the man. "Into a home. A job. Something better."

"What if God is protecting me from something worse?" Mr. Bates said. "What if this *is* my something better?"

Tony hadn't thought of it that way.

"I mean…I guess…" He wasn't sure how to answer that. "But Benny. That isn't *his* something better."

Mr. Bates shrugged again. "Sounds like he has a mother who cares. A house. A school."

Mr. Bates clearly didn't get what Tony was asking.

"Never mind."

He started at his coffee cup, feeling a bit frustrated and slightly judgmental.

"Do you feel God is letting you down?" Mr. Bates asked.

Tony looked across the table. Mr. Bates eyes were clear, penetrating.

"Not me, but Benny. And you. And that poor, scraggly kitten. Is it just luck that I'm here now, sitting in this warm café paying for coffee and sandwiches? Or is it God's providence? Did God choose whom to favor?"

"You consider yourself favored?"

Tony thought of Abigail. "Right now, definitely."

"And before?"

He thought of his grandma. "Yes. But the odds of Benny or his siblings making it out of their situation into a better life are mighty slim. You know the statistics." Or maybe he didn't. "That's why it's so important to me to figure out if this letter is real. Then they can sell it."

"Doesn't it belong to the church now? Or Walter's estate? Or some music museum?" Mr. Bates asked.

"I don't know how the law works. Maybe. But I think if Trisha had it in her possession…."

"How do you know it's not hers?"

"Well, it *is*. I'm sure the church will give it back to her."

"I mean hers for *real*."

Tony raised an eyebrow.

"I would never assume. You know what they say about assuming." Mr. Bates took a loud slurp of his coffee. "Maybe she got it from a clown."

Now he was just talking nonsense. Tony looked at his watch, then pushed his sandwich towards Mr. Bates. "Keep it for later. I told them to leave the mayo off, so it shouldn't spoil. I need to go pick up a kid."

Mr. Bates nodded, and unwrapped the sandwich. Apparently he was going to eat it now.

"Thanks," he said through a mouthful of food. Some crumbs fell onto his lap, which he didn't seem to notice.

"No problem," Tony said. "I'll let you know how the kitten is doing. Abigail will have her fattened up in no time."

He picked up Benny promptly at 9 a.m. Trisha looked as frazzled and exhausted as she had before. Benny had a huge smile on his face.

"This is *so cool!*" he said. "I get to hang out with a thief!"

"An *ex*-thief," Tony said. "I'm reformed."

"You're what?" Benny asked.

"Reformed."

"Whatever. I have this really cool mask I want to show you, and I'm super good at tracking. Me and Hershey track things all the time. Maybe I can help you today? Mom said you have to work. I'm a really hard worker. Can we break into a jewelry store?"

Benny talked all the way out the front door and into the car. Tony started up the car, and Benny immediately started playing with the radio stations.

"What is that crap you're listening to?" Benny asked.

"Does your mother allow you to stay that word?"

"What? *Crap?* Mom isn't here." Benny said.

"I see. Well, it happens to be Mozart."

"Let's listen to country. That's what my mom likes." He flipped the stations until he found one he liked, then turned it up really loud. Tony reached over and turned it down.

"The driver has to think," Tony said. And he had to get to a client meeting this morning. But what to do with the boy?

"Are you hungry?"

"I'm starved!" Benny said, although the chocolate frosting at the corner of his mouth suggested otherwise.

"I'll make you a deal. I'll stop at the store and buy you some food, but then you have to sit *really* quietly while I talk to a client."

"What's a client?"

"She's someone who I am *hoping* to get some work from." Tony glanced over at Benny. He wondered if the kid could stay quiet for a half hour.

"I can help," Benny said.

"Very well," Tony said. "How about you be my apprentice?"

"What's an apprentice?"

Tony glanced at him again, then back at the road.

"You watch and learn. If you want to be *really* good at doing what I do, you have to learn the tricks of the trade."

"Do apprentices get paid?"

"No, but you get benefits."

"What are benefits?"

Tony saw a grocery store up ahead and turned into the parking lot.

"I have a really cool flashlight, and if you do well, it's yours."

"Just a flashlight?"

Tony tried to suppress a grin. This kid was something else. "It's a super *special* flashlight. Something I use in my job. It's top notch and very cool."

"Really?" Benny sounded skeptical.

"Yep."

"Well… okay."

They went in the grocery store, and Tony convinced Benny that cheese and crackers were a better snack than Twinkies, but it wasn't easy.

"And how about some milk?" Tony said, pausing at the dairy section.

"Chocolate," Benny said.

"White is better for you," Tony said. Abigail had ruined him. Only a year ago, he would have grabbed chocolate himself.

"No it's not," Benny said. "They both come from a cow."

"But chocolate milk is more like a dessert drink," Tony said.

"How so?"

Tony took one of the chocolate milks off the shelf and turned it over so he could read the ingredients. "It has high fructose corn syrup in it."

"What's that?"

"Something that makes kids hyper." Tony frowned. Now he sounded like his grandmother. Not wanting to turn into the women in his life, he tossed the chocolate milk in the basket, and got another one for him. "Chocolate milk it is."

Tony's client meeting took longer than he expected. Benny sat quietly in a chair and sipped his chocolate milk. He was watching everything with interest.

Tony was hoping to be home when Abigail came to pick up the kitten to take it to the vet so that Benny could see Lily before she left. But the woman he met with was very worried about details. She owned a significant amount of jewelry and was concerned about break-ins. She already had tight security, but she wanted Tony to help her add more.

"But is there a way to track my jewelry if it's stolen?" she asked.

"Each individual piece?" Tony rubbed his temple. He was beginning to get a headache. This was the difference between a life of crime and a legitimate job. When he was stealing on the side, he got to pick and choose who he worked with. Now he just had to pay the bills.

"Yes," she said. "Like…can you put a tracer on my diamond earrings?"

Tony took a slow deep breath and assured her that wasn't necessary because the system he would install would deter all crime. "*All* criminal activities," he emphasized. "Nobody will be able to get through it. Ever."

He knew he shouldn't make such promises, but he felt pretty confident it was true.

"I see…" She leaned back in her expensively upholstered armchair and thought for a moment. "But what about if I'm wearing them out?"

She had a point.

By the time Tony was finished and had taken the measurements to write up an estimate for her, he was starving. Once they were back in the car, the chattering started up again.

"Did I do good?"

"You did very good."

"Do I get my flashlight?"

"Yes, you do."

"When? Where do you live? Do you work in a bat cave? Is Abigail home?"

"Why don't we turn the radio back on?" Tony said.

Tony bought them both lunch at a fast food burger joint, then took the kid to his office, an apartment not far from their home. It was full of high-tech equipment, and he figured Benny would find it fascinating. He also knew there was a special flashlight in his desk drawer that Benny would like.

"Here," he said, opening the drawer and pulling out the flashlight. It was a small, compact light, which fit neatly into a jacket pocket, but it was bright. It also had a black light bulb and a switch that changed it from one to the other.

"Look," Tony said, switching it to blacklight mode and shining it towards the countertop in the kitchen, where he knew the caulk would glow. Then he got up and walked it to his bedroom, where he had written REDRUM on the wall for a joke when he first got the light. It glowed.

"Wow!" Benny breathed. "What does that say?"

"Red room."

Benny scrutinized it. "It's spelled wrong."

"Not really. It's from a movie."

"Can I watch it?"

"No."

"Why not?"

"See what else glows," Tony said, "and write a list here. I need to know."

While Benny explored with his new light and a list, Tony booted up his computer and decided to see if he could track down Trisha's relatives. Mr. Bates had made him think.

He did a simple search on Patricia Borgnine. There were a lot of them. So he narrowed it down to her current city, and found a cell phone attached to her. Her father's name was listed in the White Pages search, but he ignored that since the angel ornament came from Trisha's mom's side of the family.

She had told him her grandma's name was Ida Brown. He typed in the name, and found seven listed. He searched for an obituary, and found her in a small town in northern Pennsylvania. Interestingly, that's where Walter was from.

So when Walter died, or maybe when he moved or something, he sold the ornament at a garage sale.

And Ida picked it up.

Or…

Tony switched software programs. The VPN would mask his IP address from any traces. Then he deftly and quickly hacked into the records department in the town in Pennsylvania where Ida was born. Brown was her married name, but with some searching her found her birth records. She was the daughter of Ellie Carlyle, who was the daughter of Nanette Burgis.

Tony decided to trace the maternal line first, because in theory mothers usually passed things on down to their daughters. Men didn't hold onto things as much. At least he didn't.

He'd start with Nanette, because that's as far back as the records went in this system. Burgis was Nanette's married name. To find her married name, he had to locate her marriage license. He glanced at the clock. He had to meet another client in twenty minutes.

It only took ten to find Nanette's marriage license. Her maiden name was…Hall.

Walter Hall was Trisha's great uncle.

Chapter Six

Abigail came home on her lunch hour to take the kitten in for a vet check. She didn't want it in hanging out with Cocoa until she knew it was healthy.

Cocoa greeted her at the door, meowing loudly. From the box, she heard the tiny mews of the kitten.

"Hello girls!" she said, bending down to scratch Cocoa behind the ears. The cat carrier was on the coffee table. Tony had remembered to dig it out of the basement for her.

Abigail gave Cocoa a treat so she didn't feel neglected, then she picked up the kitten and put her in the carrier. Purring started immediately.

"You have no idea where you're going, do you?" she said to Lily. "Innocence is bliss."

The vet's office was decorated for Christmas, with bulbs strung on tinsel above the check-in desk, and a Christmas tree in the corner containing all cat- and dog-themed ornaments.

The kitten checked out fine, and the vet gave her the required shots. She also took a blood test to be sure Lily didn't carry feline leukemia or anything else that could be contagious to Cocoa.

"She looks to be about ten weeks old," the vet said. "Have you called around to see if you can find her owner?"

"I have," Abigail said. "The homeless man said he found her in an alley."

"Probably true. I'm sure there are enough of them out there lurking through the garbage bins."

Abigail took the kitten back home and got her settled in her box. Cocoa walked around the outside of the box and hissed a few times, just to be sure Lily knew her place.

"As soon as we get finalized bloodwork back, I'm going to introduce the two of you," Abigail said. She looked down at her tortoiseshell. "Get ready to cuddle."

Cocoa meowed a loud protest.

Abigail then grabbed her handbag and drove to the appraiser's shop. She would stop in there before she returned to work.

Arvard's Antiques was located on State Street in an old building sandwiched in between a coin shop and Buffy's Burgers. The door was painted green with a gold lion's head handle, and reminded Abigail of something out of a book. She had come to Arvard before to ask him about some of the items she got in the library. He was very wise in the ways of antique documents, books, and letters.

"Abigail!" his hearty voice boomed through the store as she walked in. There was always a prevailing musty odor, and she picked her way through the clutter of old chairs, stacks of books, and antique dinner plates. Arvard was standing behind a glass counter that contained costume jewelry and baseball cards.

"Arvard, good to see you!" she said.

He was a stout man in his fifties, with short grey curly hair and wire spectacles. His stomach protruded over the brown leather belt of his khaki's, but his red shirt was neatly tucked in. Today she thought he resembled Santa Claus.

She set her bag down on his desk and carefully pulled out a leather case containing the letter, still shrouded in the archival plastic.

"What do you have here?" he said, scooting his glasses down on his nose and bending over to peer at the letter.

"You tell me," she said.

Arvard was quiet for a good long, three minutes, gazing at the letter. Then he reached to pick it up.

"May I?" he asked, peering up at her over his spectacles.

"Yes."

He picked it up and took a magnifying glass out of his drawer. He gazed some more.

"Handwriting with a fountain pen. I'd say circa late 1940s by the weave in the paper. It's the right time frame to be...."

His voice trailed off.

"To be..?" Abigail was curious as to what he would say.

Arvard slowly raised his head until their eyes met. "Authentic," he said quietly and reverently.

She couldn't stop the smile that came to her lips.

"But I need to check it to be sure," he said. "Give me a minute. Do you have time to wait?"

"Yes."

He set the letter down on the counter in front of her and hurried into the back room. She heard him whistling, and he returned with a large book, two folders, and a miniature briefcase. He opened the briefcase. Inside was another magnifying glass, this one a flat rectangle. He laid it out on the counter, placing it carefully over the letter.

Then he opened one of the folders.

"I have here a copy of an original hand-written hymn by Walter Hall. Not one of the famous ones. But it will be a good comparison."

Arvard was skilled at handwriting comparisons. She watched as he looked back and forth from one to the other.

"See here how he shapes his 's' and the loops on his 'l's here in the song's title? And how he crosses his 't's. They match."

Abigail peered down at the sheet, their heads almost touching. "I see it."

"And this looks like the same pen. There was a small leak in it. It doesn't write smoothly. Look here. Same thing. This song was written shortly before this letter, I imagine. The song is dated 1947. He probably used the same pen."

Arvard looked up. "I'd say this is a genuine letter you have here."

The two of them looked from each other, back down at the letter, and both sighed. Abigail didn't know of anyone else who got as excited over discovering a piece of history as she did, except for Arvard.

"What do we do?" she asked.

"Well, who does it belong to? It's probably worth a small fortune."

Before Abigail could answer, Arvard held up a finger for her to wait, and started flipping through a Rolodex file. "Here," he said, and picked up his cell, punching in numbers.

She heard a voice answer on the other end.

"Yeah, it's Arvard. I've got something here, and I need a price quote."

Arvard started pacing as he told the voice on the other end some details. After a few minutes, he hung up.

"He's an appraiser friend of mine, an antiques dealer in New York," he said. "We swap wares from time to time, and I see him at shows. He's going to do a bit of research on what this is worth."

"Seriously?"

"Yep."

"And I can probably find you a buyer. I know several collectors of Walter Hall's work."

Abigail picked the letter up, enclosing it in the leather case, and carefully put it back in her bag.

"Awesome. Thanks!"

"Let me look into some things," Arvard said, taking of his glasses and polishing them with a hankie. "I'll let you know how it turns out."

The snow was still falling. It had snowed steadily now for two days in a row, but it was coming down slow enough that the road crews could keep up with it and the streets were clean. The large white flakes drifted down onto her windshield, and the blades made soft hypnotic swishy sounds as they wiped the windshield clean.

As Abigail drove back to work, she thought about Walter and his love letter. He must have written it right before his wife died. And what a love story they must have had! She could imagine him walking into the store and seeing this beautiful woman, and deciding right there that she was the woman he wanted to marry.

And then losing her.

They had been married a long time. She wondered why they never had children. Maybe they couldn't? But they had had many years together, and they were happy ones, gathering from the strong love in the letter and in his Christmas song. So he had probably bought this angel to give to her for Christmas, and then she had died before she opened the gift. Because she had died on Christmas Eve.

Walter had never written another song after "My Christmas Eve Angel." He had lived a few short more years, and then he too had died. Abigail guessed from a broken heart.

She knew what it was like to lose a spouse. Nick had died after only four months of marriage. They were still newlyweds, still getting to know one another. But she already knew that he was her one true love. He had died on a cold, icy night when someone had run a stop sign and plowed into his car.

After his death, she had become somewhat of a recluse, going to work then coming home, hardly ever going out with her friends. She had sworn off love, because it hurt so much to lose someone. Her heart went out to Walter, and his suffering of long ago when he lost Angela. And his death shortly after that.

It had been six long years that she had withdrawn into herself. Years of avoiding relationships, and swearing she would never love again.

And then she had met Tony.

Tony had surprised her, quite literally with his sudden appearance in her library, and on a deeper level when he so quickly worked his way into her closed heart. She began to realize that maybe she *could* love again after all.

And now, she couldn't imagine life without him.

Sometimes she was afraid she would lose him too, and whenever that possibility crept into her mind, as it did now with thinking about Walter's story, she closed off the thoughts. She had mentioned this fear to her friend and coworker Pauline once.

"I hope nothing happens to Tony," she had said during their lunchbreak one day. She said it causally, but inside her heart was clenched in fear because she had tried calling Tony twice that morning and he hadn't answered her yet.

"He'll be fine," Pauline had said. "God would never take two men from you. That would be cruel."

But Abigail knew there were no guarantees in life. That's why both she and Tony lived life to the fullest, and why every single day she told him she loved him.

She pulled into the library parking lot and shook the thoughts from her head. She had better things to think about, like how excited Trisha and her kids would be when Abigail told them how much that letter was worth. She decided to call Tony and tell him what she had learned from Arvard.

Chapter Seven

Tony was back home after dropping Benny off with the other sitter. He was humming as he booted up his laptop. Abigail's call had put him in a good mood. The letter was original, was most likely worth quite a bit, and Arvard probably had a seller for them. All he had to do now was call the church and see if they would be willing to let the letter go back to Trisha.

It was, after all, legally hers, even if she had "given" it to the church. He had no fears that Naomi would have a problem with any of this. Her heart was golden. He gave her a quick call and just as he thought, the church wasn't intending to keep it. It was Trisha's if she wanted it.

Tony heard a loud hiss from the front room. "What's going on in there?" He got up from the kitchen table where he had been working with his laptop, and went to see. Cocoa was standing on the back of the couch and looking down into the box. Her hair was raised, her back arched, and she was standing on her toes.

"Hissssssssss!" she said again.

Tony heard a pathetic mew from inside the box.

"Girls, you need to get along," he said.

He went back into the kitchen and returned with a bag of cat treats. He gave one to Cocoa, who reluctantly came out of "attack" mode to eat it, and he handed another one down to Lily in her box. The kitten was curled up on the towel that Abigail had put in for a bed. She also had added a small metal tin full of litter for Lily's potty.

"Hey," Tony said, taking a closer look at the make-shift litter box. "That's our metal cake pan!"

It was the nineteen-incher. The one Abigail made her delicious pineapple upside down cakes in.

"Lily, what *are* we going to do with you?" He glanced at Cocoa. She didn't seem at all happy with this new addition. Tony hadn't talked to Abigail about Lily's future. Did she want to keep the kitten?

What if they gave it to Benny? That little boy needed something to cuddle. He remembered seeing how much he hugged his dog. And Tony hadn't seen any Christmas presents, nor a tree. What if he gave the kitten to the mom to give to the kids? He'd have to supply them with food and litter, of course. Until they got the money from the sale of Walter's letter.

The more he thought of it, the more he liked the idea of Lily the Christmas kitten going to stay with the Borgnines.

He figured he should check all of this out with Mr. Bates. He had, after all, told him he'd let him know how Lily was doing. He'd pay him a second visit today.

Tony had to meet a client, so he left early to stop by the shelter. He went up and knocked on the door, and an older gentleman opened it. He had several front teeth missing, and was munching on a fruit bar.

"I'm here to see Mr. Bates," Tony said.

The man chewed for a moment, watching him thoughtfully, but didn't speak. Tony peered past him. "Can I come in?" Tony asked.

The man simply stepped aside, still chewing.

The shelter was clean and smelled of disinfectant. It appeared to be a large room, like a gymnasium, and in the back he could see a kitchen area. There were several beds lining both sides of the walls, some with men sitting on them reading, doing crosswords, or sleeping. Other beds were empty. Tony didn't see Mr. Bates, so he wandered through to the back. Beside the kitchen there was a hallway and he went through that to find Mr. Bates in a smaller room that had large windows. Several folding chairs had been pulled over near the window, and he was sitting in one, looking out. His coat was off and slug over the back of his chair, and his back was to Tony, his shoulders sagging. A slant of weak sunlight was streaming through the snow outside and highlighting the top of his silver hair.

"Mr. Bates?" Tony said. The man didn't move at first, then slowly turned. He smiled acknowledgement and motioned for Tony to sit in the chair next to him.

Cut-out paper snowflakes and children's drawings of angels and Christmas trees decorated the room. Tony wondered if a church or school made them as a service to the shelter.

"Abigail took Lily to the vet for a checkup," Tony said. "She's healthy, and she's getting fat on the food Abigail is feeding her. She bought her these little cans of gourmet kitten food."

As Tony said that, he wondered if it might have been better for them to buy food for Mr. Bates and get him a physical. If he was remembering right, he thought there was a health clinic not far from here. But he had no idea how to begin without offending him. "Do you need a doctor?" seemed inappropriate, when the man didn't seem sick.

"I came to update you on the kitten," Tony said instead.

He could hear a radio station on in the kitchen and strands of 'White Christmas' reached his ears.

Mr. Bates turned to Tony. "Do you have family? Other than Abigail, I mean?"

"Yes. I have my grandma," Tony said. "She raised me."

Mr. Bates nodded. "Sounds like a good woman."

"She is."

"Prays a lot."

Tony nodded. It seemed an odd thing to say.

"Gary," the man finally said. "My name is Gary Bates. As for family…" Gary Bates got quiet for a minute, turned back to the window. 'White Christmas' had ended and Walter's song 'My Christmas Eve Angel' started up. Tony wondered who got the royalties every time that song was played. "No family. Not here, anyway."

Tony waited for more of an explanation, but none came. Gary Bates was a man of few words.

Tony stood. "Well," he said, rubbing his hands up and down his arms to warm them up, "I just came to tell you that Lily is okay and when you're ready for her, we can bring her back."

"The shelter doesn't allow animals," he said. "Why don't you keep her?"

Tony nodded. "I suspect Abigail would like that. Or I had in mind a family of children that might like her. The family I told you about this morning."

Gary smiled up at Tony. "Lily would like that, to be with kids."

"Then it's set. Lily will have a home with children. Do you need anything?"

Mr. Bates shook his head. "I have everything I need, Tony. Thank you." He reached his hand out, and Tony shook it. "It was nice to meet you. You're a good man."

Tony held his blue eyes for a moment, and felt for a second as if he was looking into a man much older. But the moment quickly passed and he turned to leave. As he walked out into the snow, he couldn't help but feel like Mr. Bates was saying a final goodbye.

Chapter Eight

Abigail was telling Pauline about Benny's family and their needs. She had already told Pauline about the letter from Walter, but she still hadn't heard back from the appraiser.

"Meanwhile, the kids look like they're freezing," she said. "Tony said Benny's pants were too short and his jacket was thin."

"I've kept the kids clothes in tubs in the garages," Pauline said. "I have no idea why. We don't plan to have more. I'll go through them tonight. I know I have plenty for the baby, and maybe a few winter coats. Why don't you stop by after dinner, around 7:30 and pick them up?"

Abigail said she would and went to get her coat. There was a storm heading into town, and she wanted to get home before she got caught in it. It was only 5 p.m., but it was dark outside. That was one of the problems of living in Michigan—the long, dark, cold days in winter. She missed the sun.

She descended the front steps, jiggling her keys in her hand, and briefly turned her face up into the large snowflakes that were falling all around her. She tasted a few, but needed to get home. She had driven to work today, and hoped the roads were still good. Fortunately, she only had to go across town.

Then she saw him. He was sitting in the same place he had been the other night. Mr. Bates was huddled on the steps, his big grey coat bundled around him, his toboggan cap pulled nearly over his eyes. As she approached him, she heard him humming a little tune. It was Walter's angel song. He saw her and smiled.

"Abigail, I came to thank you for taking care of Lily," he said.

"Oh, no worries," she said. "She's really sweet."

"Tony said he was thinking of giving her to the Borgnine family."

"He did?" She swallowed. "Um, that's a great idea!" She forced a smile. She had to admit, a part of her wanted to keep the kitten. She hadn't even really considered giving her away. She'd teach Cocoa and Lily to get along.

"I think it is. Lily will love being with children. Kittens are great for kids, especially when they're going through stuff. The divorce has been hard on Benny. He has lost his trust in men. I think when Tony delivers the kitten, it'll help."

She thought about that. Tony was so good at making people feel worthy and loved. What better idea then to take the kitten with him when they brought Pauline's clothes over tonight? She knew the family needed that little cat more than she did. She imagined the smiles on the kids' faces. Mr. Bates and Tony must have had quite the talk today.

The snow was coming down harder. She would have inches on her car by now that would need to be brushed off. Suddenly, she was anxious to get home.

"Do you need anything?" she asked. "A ride back to the shelter?"

"I have everything I need," Mr. Bates said.

She was glad he hadn't accepted the offer. She was still unsure about being alone with him.

The ride home wasn't too bad. The plow trucks were already out, keeping ahead of it. She stepped through the front door and shook the snow from her long, red hair.

"Hello, beautiful," Tony said, coming to give her a kiss.

"Hi, handsome."

"Shall I compare these to a summer's day?"

"Ooooh, a sonnet!" She smiled and wrapped her arms around him, kissing him again. This one was a bit lingering.

"Do you want to skip dinner and go straight for dessert?" he teased.

"That sounds fun," she said, pulling reluctantly away and taking her coat off. Then her stomach growled. "But I'm starved and it smells so good!" She reached into the cardboard box and scratched Lily on the head.

Tony had stir-fried some vegetables and chicken, and put them over rice. Abigail sat down to the warm, spicy meal. Cocoa, who had greeted her at the door, rubbed against her legs, hoping for a piece of chicken.

"It has sauce on it," Abigail said. "Not good for kitties."

Cocoa gave her a plaintive meow.

Tony told her about his day, and about learning Mr. Bates first name.

"That's funny you saw Mr. Bates. I did too," Abigail said. "He was sitting outside the library when I left. We discussed Lily." She looked towards the box, her heart breaking just a bit. "He thinks giving her to Trisha and her family is a good idea. I mean, if we take food over, and pay for her first vet bills…"

"That's exactly what I was thinking!" Tony said. His eyes lit up. "We can buy cat food and a litter box and give them a whole package deal!" But then his eyes narrowed. "Are you willing to give her up? I mean, I know how attached you can get."

Abigail sighed. "I know. But he's right. She'll be good for them. He thinks the divorce was hard on the kids. Even though their dad is a jerk and they never see him, he's still their dad." She took a bite of rice, chewed, and thought. "You and him must have had quite a talk, because he knew quite a bit about them."

"I didn't tell him much," Tony said.

"Just about the divorce and all?"

Tony shook his head. "No, I said they were split, but I never mentioned the divorce. He could have assumed. But I know I never told him Benny's name…" his eyes narrowed. "You didn't?"

Abigail put her fork down. "No."

They sat and looked at each other for a moment.

Finally Abigail said, in a very quiet voice, "He was humming 'My Christmas Eve Angel' when I found him."

Tony jumped up and went in to the next room. He returned with his laptop.

"Let me see what I can find on him."

Abigail left her plate and went around the table. She pulled up a chair next to Tony.

Tony typed in his name.

"There are a few Gary Bates on here…" he said, pointing to the list that came up on Google. "Let's narrow the search. How old do you think he is?"

Abigail shrugged. "I don't know. 50s? Maybe 60s? Probably 60s."

"And we'll plug in the location."

He found the names in the White Pages, but it wasn't any help.

"I doubt he has a phone we can trace him by," Abigail said. "And we know he doesn't have an address."

"We need to get the big guns out," Tony said. He looked at her.

"Okay," she said, standing. "Let me put the food away and we'll go. This would also be a good time to drop the clothes off at Trisha's house."

Abigail pulled her coat tighter around her, and wished the car would heat up faster. The snow was really blowing, but the streets were clear. She refrained from saying anything about the weather.

She hated nights like these, and was afraid to drive in them, but she knew that if she suggested staying in, Tony would counter with "We live in Michigan. It snows all the time." And he was right.

Besides, Tony's apartment was only a five-minute-drive from their house. He had kept it after they got married, and used it as an office where he met with clients.

He unlocked the doors, and went in and booted up the computers. Abigail went and turned up the heat.

After a few minutes, Tony logged onto his computer, and opened up some specialty software.

"I assume you're okay with me cyber-stalking him a bit, or you wouldn't be here?"

She nodded and pulled a chair up beside him. "Yep. I'm a bit freaked out by him, if you want the truth."

She had never really felt that Mr. Bates was a threat, but he knew too much about them. She had learned not to trust what she saw. People weren't always who they seemed.

Tony started a random search on the name.

"We don't even know if that's his real name," he said.

Hundreds of Gary Bates popped up in the United States. Then he narrowed them by age and state. They were down to five living in Michigan.

He hacked into the Secretary of State and into the driver's license department.

Abigail looked over at him. "That was fast."

"I…let's just say I needed to get in here about a week ago. They haven't changed their security."

She chose not to think about that.

Five photos of Gary Bates appeared. None of them were their guy.

Tony closed out that system and plugged in his phone. A photo of Tony smiling with Mr. Bates appeared.

"You took a selfie with him?" Abigail exclaimed. Although at this point, nothing should surprise her.

"Yeah, why not?" Tony said. "Besides, it's always good to have a few photos of the people you interact with. You never know when you're going to need them."

Good point. But she shook her head.

"*Be still prepared for death: and death or life shall thereby be the sweeter,*" he mumbled, his fingers flying across the keyboard.

She thought about that. Another Shakespeare quote, and she had no idea where it came from. She counted the points on her fingers. She was losing their quote game, so she decided to distract him. "This moment called for quote on preparedness and all you can come up with is one on death?" she teased.

"You have anything better?"

"*By failing to prepare, you are preparing to fail.*"

"Benjamin Franklin. My point." Tony said. "Ha!"

"That's hardly fair. Everyone knows Benjamin Franklin quotes."

"Maybe you should read more Shakespeare."

She elbowed him in the ribs. His computer had scanned the photo and was running through a database, trying to match it.

"When should we give them the kitten?"

"I say we take it over on Christmas morning. We'll tell Trisha and see if that works."

Abigail imagined the kids opening a box on Christmas morning with Lily inside. "I like that," she said.

"He doesn't exist," Tony said.

"What?"

"He doesn't exist."

Abigail stared at the computer's red font saying "No Matches Found."

"He's homeless," she said. "Probably no record of him. I mean, if he never got a driver's license or an ID, he wouldn't be in the system."

"Who doesn't have an ID? I have three or four."

"Very funny, cat burglar."

Tony sat back in his chair, twirling a little bit and staring at the screen. She could tell he was thinking. Finally he turned to her. "I think we're paranoid," he said. "I mean, he's just a homeless dude. Not a criminal. That's probably not even his real name, just something he made up. Let's go take those clothes to Trisha."

"You're right," Abigail said. "We *are* paranoid. But who can blame us after all the shenanigans we've been through?" Living with Tony and his checkered past had taught her to always be suspicious of people she met. Her work, too, had taught her to be careful. Some people would go to great lengths to get their hands on an old document. Money made people do all sorts of crazy things.

The storm was coming. The snow was increasing, but the roads were still okay. They briefly stopped by Pauline's house, and then Tony drove them towards the bridge and the other side of town, the big tub of clothes in the trunk. She hoped they made it home before the storm fully hit.

Chapter Nine

Tony could hear the baby crying as soon as they got out of the car. He opened the trunk and lifted out the tub.

"This is where they live?" Abigail said.

"Yep."

Someone had drawn some Christmas pictures in crayon and they were taped on the door for decorations. They heard shouting inside, from one of the kids. Abigail knocked.

Trisha opened the door, with the baby on her hip. When he saw them, he stopped crying. His lip was out, and tears streaked his face.

"Hi!" Trisha said, forcing a smile, but her eyes were bright with unshed tears. Tony saw the dark circles under her eyes. "Come in."

Benny was standing behind her, tears running down his cheeks.

"This is *your* fault!" he said to his mother, apparently not done with the shouting. *"It's all your fault!* I hate you, and I don't want to live here anymore!" He ran to his room and slammed the door shut.

"Is this a bad time?" Abigail asked. "We brought over some clothes. I can leave them here."

Tony stepped inside and looked for a clean spot on the floor, but there wasn't one. He slid some toys out of the way with his boot to clear a space, and set the tub down. Hershey came over to him, wiggling her butt and wanting to be petted.

"The house is a mess," Trisha said. "I'm sorry, I was trying to get the laundry done."

The house *was* a mess. Piles of clothes were scattered across the floor. Abigail stepped into the house, but just as she did, Benny came running out of his room, nearly knocking her and Tony down on his way to the front door. Tears streaked his red face. He had his coat on.

"Benny? Where are you going?" Trisha shouted.

"I'm going to go see Dad!" Benny shouted. He pulled his boots on. Pushing past Abigail, he ran out the door.

"Benny! You get back here right now!"

But Benny was running, shining his flashlight in front of him. Quickly, before the door swung shut, Hershey bolted after Benny.

"Grab her!" Trisha said.

Tony made a reach for her, but the dog was too fast.

Then Trisha gasped.

They looked in the direction she was staring. Benny was barreling towards the street, the dog at his heels, and there was a car coming. In his rage, Benny didn't see the car. Trisha screamed his name. The car was going to hit him.

"Benny, stop!" Tony yelled, but the driver saw Benny in time, and swerved, ending up in the ditch. Immediately, he opened his window and peeked behind him, cursing. He started spinning his tires.

"Benny, come back here!" Trisha yelled, her desperate voice startling Henry. The baby started to cry again, screaming loud wails. Benny and the dog had crossed the street and disappeared in between some houses. They were no longer in sight.

Trisha smoothed the baby's hair. "Poor Henry is tired. I just told Benny his dad isn't coming for Christmas. Darren wouldn't even talk to the kids when I called him to ask. Benny is shattered." She peered out into the darkness, juggling the baby on her hip. Her little girl came to stand beside her. She was crying too. "Benny's going to get himself killed," Trisha said.

"We'll go find him," Abigail said, looking at Tony. She meant that *he* would go find them.

"Yep," Tony said. Because what else was there to do? His heart went out to the boy. There was a storm coming and the kid would freeze with his thin coat. "Let's drive," Tony said. He turned to Trisha. "We'll be right back."

"Please find him," Trisha said, looking up at the dark sky. "It's so cold. That darn kid never listens. And he's really upset."

Abigail followed Tony out to the car, and he headed in the direction the kid had gone.

"I hate kids," he said.

"No you don't," Abigail said.

"No, I *don't*. But maybe this particular one. Just a little."

Abigail smiled. Tony turned down a side street and caught a glimpse of Benny chasing the dog between two houses.

"They're headed towards the river," Abigail said.

Tony took a side street in that direction.

Then, up ahead, he saw them. Benny waving his flashlight and running frantically north, the big dog loping beside him. It took a minute for him to get his bearings, but he realized if Benny kept heading in the same direction, he was soon going to be on ice.

"He can't see the river because the snow is so deep," Abigail said, at the same time Tony realized it.

Tony's heart started racing. The river wouldn't be frozen through—it hardly ever was. He honked his horn, but in this wind, he doubted if Benny could hear him. He pushed down the accelerator, and sped down the little street, heading toward the boy and his dog.

"Benny!" Abigail had rolled down her window and was shouting. But Benny kept running, pushed forward by emotion. He crossed the street, went down a slope, and then he was on the river, still running.

Tony reached the edge of the river and stopped the car so fast it slid into a 180. Once it settled, he jumped out.

"Benny!" he shouted. "Benny, stop! You're on the river! The ice is thin!"

Benny heard him and stopped running. He turned. The dog stopped and pressed her body up against the boy's leg, her tongue hanging out.

"Go away!" Benny shouted. "I'm going to go find my dad!"

"Your dad is far away," Tony shouted. "You need a car! Come on, I'll drive you!"

He didn't usually lie, but he had to get the kid off the ice. Heck, maybe he *would* drive the kid to see his dad. He'd like to give the jerk a piece of his mind.

"You will?" Benny's voice carried over the expanse.

The lights from the bridge cast a glow down below onto the ice, and Tony could see Benny's face. He looked hopeful. "You promise?"

"I promise," Tony said. "Just walk towards me *really slowly*. The ice is thin."

Benny suddenly realized where he was. Fear filled his eyes as he cast his light down on the snow-covered ice in front of him.

"Tony!" he said, the terror in his voice carrying across the ice.

"I know. You're fine. Just move slow."

Then they heard a sickening cracking sound. The dog sensed the danger and started to whine.

"I'll call 911," Abigail said, pulling her phone out.

They didn't have time to wait for emergency help. Tony ran towards the car and popped open the trunk. He unzipped his tool bag and pulled out a black rope. Tying it to the car bumper, he tied the other end around his waist.

"I'm going to get him," he said, running towards the river's edge.

"Tony, no!" Abigail said. "Tony!"

He heard her screaming his name, but he kept going. "Make sure the rope doesn't come untied!"

When he was on the ice he slowed down and made his way towards the boy and his dog, walking slowly, reaching his hand forward.

"Don't move," he said to Benny. "I'm coming to get you."

"Tony, I'm scared." New tears were running down Benny's face. "I don't want to die."

"Nobody's going to die tonight," Tony said. He felt the wind whipping through his coat, and felt the ice splintering under him. "Shine the flashlight in front of me," he said. "Easy."

Carefully, Benny did as he was told, but Tony couldn't see the ice through the snow.

"Keep the light on the ice in front of me. I have no idea how thick it is here," he said. "But I can hear it cracking."

He could. There was a crackling sound all around him. He hoped his rope held if he went through.

He stopped about five feet from Benny. Where the snow was pushed aside from the tracks of the dog and boy, Tony could see the ice. It was black in color and had fractures running through it. In one place he could even see the water running under it. He swallowed hard and took a deep breath to calm his fear.

"Hershey, stay," he said again, pointing at the dog. Then he reached his hand out towards Benny.

"I need you to come one at a time. Benny, slowly come here."

Benny took a small step. "Tony, I'm scared."

"Me too," Tony said. "Just move slowly. Here. Look at me. Look at my eyes. Don't look anywhere else."

Benny's big dark eyes raised to Tony's. He saw the fear deep in the kid, and felt his own hands shaking. If they made it out of this alive it would be a miracle. The ice cracked some more.

"Take another small step," Tony said. Or would it be better if the kid laid down flat and crawled? That would spread his weight out. But what about the dog?

"Come on," Tony said. "Take another small step." But Benny had frozen. He started to cry more. "I can't do it. I can't do it, Tony!"

"Yes, you can," Tony said. Hershey whined, wanting to come, but stayed put as told. She was a good dog. The storm was violent now, the wind brutal and the snow falling hard.

"Benny, keep looking at me," Tony said, shouting over the wind. The kid met his eyes again. "Do you want to know what Abigail and I got you for Christmas?"

Benny sniffed. "You got me a *present?*"

Tony nodded. "Take another step and I'll tell you."

Just then Hershey decided to crawl. She scooted her belly towards Benny, but the boy didn't notice. "What did you get me?" he said. Tentatively, he took another small step.

"Well," Tony said. Hershey was almost even with Benny now. "I got you something sweet."

"Candy?"

"Sweeter," Tony said. Just then, the ice gave way with a deadly snap, and Benny's right leg went through. His eyes registered surprise, just before the rest broke, pulling him and the dog down together. They resurfaced briefly, with Benny's hand grasping for Hershey's collar, then they both went under, pulled by the current.

"Benny!" Tony shouted, and found he was cursing. Without thinking, he ran towards the hole, intending to reach in, but the ice broke away in large chunks all around him. He felt icy water gushing into his left boot milliseconds before a hole opened up under him and he fell through. The cold made him gasp, and he inhaled a large amount of icy water into his lungs. He came up for breath, trying to cough the water out, feeling his limbs going numb. He heard Abigail screaming from the side of the river before the dark water swallowed him under.

Chapter Ten

Panic washed over Abigail as she saw first Benny, and then Tony fall through the ice. She was screaming, and for a moment thought she was going to vomit. She realized she needed to do something, but she couldn't think. Then she saw the rope and grabbed it. It was still tied to the car bumper. She gave a firm, steady pull, praying, *begging* God that Tony wasn't already dead from inhaling water. But the rope went slack, and she pulled up nothing.

"*Tony!* Please God, *no!*" she called, then she remembered she had been dialing 911. She looked at her phone and realized the call never went through. Her phone was dead. She had forgotten to charge it. She looked around but there was nobody there, or at least none she could see through the blizzard.

"Help!" she yelled. "Somebody, please help!" But there was no one in sight. The storm had forced people inside tonight.

She ran back to the car where the open trunk was filling with snow, and started looking through Tony's bag. There *had* to be something she could use. As she threw tools out—a knife, flashlights, a harness (why hadn't he put the harness on?) she was acutely aware of the time ticking away. Tony and Benny only had minutes, maybe *seconds*, left. A brief thought flitted through her mind that a person could only hold their breath for about three minutes before brain damage occurred.

Finding nothing, she turned back towards the river and grabbed the rope. She tied it around her waist with the best knot she could, screaming all the time for help, and checked the knot at the bumper. She'd go in after them.

She grabbed the flashlight and shone it across the river. Dark, black water churned in the middle where Tony, Benny and the dog had fallen in. The current was strong. What if they were downriver by now? Realizing the futility, Abigail dropped to her knees in agony, knowing they were lost. She shook her phone, as if sheer willpower would make it work, screaming at it. Then she remembered Tony kept a charger in the car. She jumped up, turned, and ran smack into someone.

"Help!" she screamed. "Help me, please! Call 911!"

It was then she saw who it was. In a surreal moment of displacement, it took her a minute to recognize him. Mr. Bates.

Swallowing a sob, she pushed past him to the car. If she could only get to the car. But he put a strong hand on her arm and stopped her.

She turned to beat him off, frantic, fighting with the force of a bear, beating him with her fists. What was he *doing?* What was he *thinking?*

"Let go of me!" she screamed, wondering where other help was. "Tony! Tony, please!" not knowing if she was calling her husband to help her, or if she was already mourning him. The face of Trisha flashed into her mind, and she briefly wondered how she would ever tell her she had lost a child tonight.

"God, please!" Abigail cried and prayed, but Mr. Bates had both hands on her now, one on each arm.

"Quiet, child," he said, pulling her to face him. "I'm here."

What could *he* do? He couldn't even help *himself!* Suddenly she was angry, angry at Mr. Bates, angry at God, angry at Tony for going after Benny, angry at Benny. She hated herself in this moment more than she ever had before. She hated Mr. Bates too, in a fierce, unfair way.

"Let me go!" she screamed again, but he held tight. He was strong.

"Look at me," he said. His voice was firm, filled with strength, and even though he spoke quietly, she could hear him above the wind and blowing snow. Something about the way he spoke made her stop screaming, stop struggling, and look at him.

"I'm here to help," he said. "Watch."

She could feel warmth coming from his hands. The warmth came through her coat and into her arms. She felt it envelop her, radiating up her arms to her shoulders, her face, and then spreading into her torso and down into her legs. Her whole body felt a peculiar warmth, like she had just stepped into the sunlight, and with the warmth came a deep sense of peace.

Then, softly, Mr. Bates hands began to glow. The glow crept up until he was tinged with it, like an aura. He let go of her arms, and she took a step back. She couldn't take her eyes off of him.

She watched as Mr. Bates' form started to expand. He stayed man-sized, and yet he became larger, more powerful, somehow "bigger" than he was. His coat shimmered and turned into a glowing white garment, fitting loosely around him like a robe. The features of his face transformed into a different person, a younger man, and yet his eyes were old as time. His grey hair was now golden, and his toboggan cap was gone. In its place was a bright glow, a shimmery ring of light. Muscles rippled under his tunic, and broad shoulders promised strength, with arms the size of tree logs.

Mr. Bates turned and raised his arms. Then he glided – didn't walk – towards the hole where Tony had fallen through.

Abigail watched as he held both arms out towards the dark swirling water, and a white glowing mist began to swirl upwards, like a tornado. The snow mixed in with it, and for a moment, she lost sight of him. Then the light was so bright she had to turn away.

Abigail fell to her knees on the cold ground, whether from fear or reverence she didn't know. She kept her head down, her hand in front of her face to shield the light.

Then suddenly the light faded and she heard coughing beside her.

She lifted her head and turned to her right. A figure lay on the ground near her, in the darkness. She couldn't distinguish who it was.

She just sat there for a moment, trying to take it in. The warm glow was gone. She felt the cold wind against her face, and wiped her cheek with the back of her hand. Tears.

"Tony?" she said, crawling over to the figure. Then her mind snapped back to reality and for a moment, panic seized her. "Tony!" she called, her voice frantic, and reached out to touch the coughing figure.

He rolled over. And there he was. *Tony*. Wet, coughing, sputtering, and shivering. But it was Tony! Alive!

"Hey, Beautiful," he said, looking up into her eyes.

She threw herself across him, hugging him, not caring that snow and water were seeping through her coat.

"Abigail?" Tony said, his voice rough.

"Hmmm?" Her face was against his chest, the cold, wet front of his jacket.

"Where's Benny?"

She sat bolt upright. "Benny!"

And there he was, sitting up and rubbing his face with his soggy mittens. He too, was coughing.

"Where's Hershey?" Benny said.

They looked around, and suddenly the dog was there, licking Benny in the face. Wet, but none the worse for wear. Benny laughed and threw his arms around her.

"I'm freezing," Tony said. His teeth were starting to chatter. "What? How....? Did the dog drag us out?"

"Let's get you both in the car," Abigail said. Reason was taking over now, and she got up, offering Tony a hand up. "Come on, Benny."

She put Tony in the passenger seat, and Benny and the dog in the back. Then she started the car and cranked the heat up as far as it would go.

"Can you grab my tools?" Tony asked, his teeth chattering.

They were strewn out on the ground in the snow. She nodded and got out, but that's not what she was looking for. She was looking for Mr. Bates.

"Mr. Bates?" she called. "Mr. Bates!"

The storm was in full force now. She couldn't see much in the blowing snow. She yelled, trying to raise her voice above the wind. "Mr. Bates!"

Nothing. No one answered.

She looked up at the night time sky, and watched the snow swirling above her. The realization of what had just happened sunk in. "Thank you," she whispered.

"Abigail! I think we should get Benny into some warm clothes!" Tony called from the car.

"Right!" she said, and quickly picked up Tony's tools and the rope and threw them in the trunk. She got in the car and looked over at Tony.

"You're alive," she said.

"Yeah," he said. "What happened?"

"Mr. Bates," Abigail said. "He's gone home. He had a home all along."

Chapter Eleven

"An angel," Tony said again, shaking his head. "Wow." He took another sip of the hot chocolate Abigail made, then set it on the stand next to him. It felt good to be home.

"Yep," Abigail told him. "He started to glow and pulled the three of you out of the river."

Tony couldn't remember anything after he fell through. He gasped, his lungs filled with cold water, and that's the last thing he recalled. Abigail kept insisting it was an angel who saved them. The doctors at the emergency room told her that under times of stress, your mind could play tricks on you. That the dog had probably saved them. Dogs did that. There were a lot of accounts.

They were on the couch in their living room. Abigail was sitting on his lap, with her arms around his neck. She had her face up against his chest, and his arm was around her, pulling her close. Cocoa laid beside them, purring, and he could feel the warmth of the cat's furry body against his leg. Lily had been allowed out of her box and was curled up on the other side of them. Cocoa was keeping an eye on her.

"I'm okay," he said for about the tenth time, because Abigail needed to hear it again, and because it was true. After going back to Trisha's house to let her know they found Benny and the dog, Abigail had insisted on driving them both to the hospital just to get checked out. But they were both okay, not even hypothermia.

For Benny, it had all been a grand adventure. He too didn't remember anything after falling through. But he remembered Tony going out onto the ice after him.

"I wish I had a dad like you," Benny said. "My own dad sucks."

They were sitting in the hospital ER waiting to get checked out when those words came out. Tony had looked at him, ruffled the kid's hair a bit, and said, "Your own dad might not be around, but you have a perfect dad who loves you more than you can imagine. Your heavenly father."

Benny thought about that. The kid was familiar with God because he attended church regularly. After a moment, he said, "I guess I do. I need to remember that."

"Yep," Tony said.

"Abigail says He sent us an angel."

"Yes."

"Wow," Benny said. "Why did he choose to save *us?*"

"Abigail says angels are powered by prayer. I think that you and I have a lot of people praying for us."

Then the doctor came in and checked them both out, and they took Benny home. Now Tony and Abigail were sitting on their couch in their own home, safe and warm.

And grateful.

"I thought I lost you tonight," Abigail said.

"But you didn't," Tony said, holding her closer. His Abigail. His angel. He wondered if he had another angel out there as well. It appeared he did.

A message popped in on her phone.

"Who's texting you at midnight?" Tony said.

"I'll ignore it," Abigail said, but she glanced at the coffee table where it lay. "It looks like…"

Another ping.

"Wait. It's Arvard! My appraiser."

She reached for her phone. "Oh my gosh! He says that letter is worth $350,000 and he found a buyer!"

Tony whistled. "That's fantastic!"

"We should tell Trisha!"

"Let's tell her in the morning," Tony said. "She and the kids need to get some rest."

Tony stood, lifting Abigail in his arms. He gave her a kiss. "And let's you and I do the same thing."

She smiled, and he carried her off to bed, leaving the two cats sleeping on the couch together. Abigail was asleep in minutes. He lay there on his side, his arm wrapped around Abigail, and listened to her breathing. He thanked God for his life, and for giving him more time with the woman he loved. Then he heard hissing coming from the other room.

He sighed, got up, and went into the living room.

"Girls," he said, looking at both cats. Cocoa was sitting on the couch glaring down at the kitten, and poor little Lily was hunkered on the floor, her back arched and her fur standing on end. She saw Tony and felt a bit braver, so offered up a loud hiss at Cocoa.

"Girls," he said again. "Why can't you get along?" He scooped Lily up, scratching her under the chin, and deposited her in her box. "Go to sleep." She laid on her blanket, as if she understood.

He went and climbed back into bed and put his arm around Abigail again. She stirred a little, but didn't wake. He felt the bed bounce a little bit, and then Cocoa was at his feet, curling up and keeping them warm. He smiled and drifted off to sleep to the happy purr of the cat, and the warmth of contentment.

The next day was Christmas Eve. They woke early because they wanted to take the news to Trisha before she went off to work. She only had to work until 2 p.m. but this afternoon Tony and Abigail had other plans so wanted to go over early.

The snow had stopped around midnight and the roads were clear. It looked like it was going to be a sunny day.

They pulled up to the little house and knocked on the door.

"Good morning!" Trisha greeted them with a smile on her face. They all gave hugs, now bonded through a shared gratefulness. "What are you guys doing out so early?"

"Are the kids still asleep?" Tony asked.

Trisha laughed. "No way. These guys get up at the crack of dawn."

"Tony!" Benny barreled to the doorway and embraced him in a huge bear hug. Tony hugged him back, and then they high-fived. His sister Marla came and stood shyly behind her mom.

"We have some news," Abigail said. She had talked to the appraiser this morning and was so excited to share.

"Remember the angel tree topper you donated to the church?"

Trisha nodded.

"Well, that angel is about to change your life!"

Tony chuckled at Abigail's presentation. She was as excited as a kid on Christmas. He watched Trisha's face as Abigail told her the news. It transformed from disbelief to shock to tears. Soon she was hugging them, and everybody was crying.

Well, Tony wasn't. He would never cry. At least not publicly.

"So we're like...*rich?*" Benny asked, his eyes wide.

"You're rich," Tony said. "And we have something else for you."

He went outside and jogged back to the car. Abigail had talked to Trisha last night about this so he knew it was okay.

Tony picked up the small box and brought it inside. Abigail had wrapped it with tissue and a bow. There was a plaintive meowing from inside.

"What is it?" Benny asked.

"Open it," Tony said. "Remember I promised to give you something?"

"Yeah. You said something *sweet*."

"It doesn't get much sweeter than this," Abigail said.

Marla was jumping up and down, her hands clasped. Tony set the box down on the floor, and both kids sat down beside it.

"Be gentle," Tony said.

They started carefully unwrapping the box. When Benny popped the top open, Lily popped her head out.

"A kitten!" Marla said, laughing. She picked her up and hugged her, then handed her to Benny. He hugged her too. Lily purred and spatted at Marla's pigtail. Benny put her down and rolled a small ball across the floor. She ran after it and pounced.

Hershey lifted her head up from her nap and watched the kitten as Benny and Marla played. Eventually, Lily saw Hershey, and walked tentatively over. She stopped about a foot from the dog, and arched her back, dancing on her toes. Hershey didn't seem to care. Lily danced around for a moment, then seemed to think this large creature was okay. She laid down, right next to her big paws. Hershey put her head back down, her nose against the kitten, and they both went to sleep.

"I guess that worked out," Tony said. He handed Trisha a bag. "Cat food and litter. She's already had her vet check and her first shots. So you're all set until you get the check from that letter, which Abigail will pick up for you the day after Christmas."

"Thank you," Trisha said. "Thank you both so much."

"Don't thank us," Abigail said. "Thank *Him*." She glanced upwards. "He made all of this possible."

"He certainly did," Trisha said. "I guess we really do have angels watching over us."

***

On the way home, Tony wanted to stop by the homeless shelter to see if Mr. Bates had left anything.

"Who?" the manager at the homeless shelter said.

"His name was Gary Bates," Tony said. "He was a big guy. Tall, broad. Probably in his sixties."

"I don't think we have anyone by that name here."

"I'll show you a photo." Tony pulled open his photos on his phone and scanned through them. There were a few pictures of the kitten, but nothing else recent. The photo he had taken of Mr. Bates was gone.

"Did you delete it?" Abigail asked.

"No. I don't think so."

Tony and Abigail asked to come inside. Tony stopped at the front desk, where he had signed the man in.

"Yeah, I remember you," said the woman behind the desk. Her voice was gravelly from smoking. "But I never saw the guy you said you brought with you."

Tony remembered Mr. Bates wandering into the next room as Tony was signing him in.

"Big guy," he said, and described him.

She shook her head. "Never saw him. He never showed up. But you're welcome to ask around."

They walked through the shelter and asked a few people who were awake. None had ever seen Mr. Bates and the shelter worker who had originally taken him in didn't seem to work there. And never had.

On the way out, Tony told Abigail about the coffee shop.

"Let's stop there," Tony said.

"I don't think you'll find anything," Abigail said.

She was right. None of the workers remembered seeing Tony come in with anybody.

"Let me ask Pauline," Abigail said. "He was in the library a few times."

She called her coworker.

"Merry Christmas Eve!" Pauline said.

Abigail wished her the same. "Hey, do you remember the big homeless guy who has been in the library a few times? Grey coat?"

"Hmmmm," Pauline said. "No big guys. I remember the woman you snuck in a few times when Ms. Scott wasn't looking." She laughed. "And that really skinny dude."

"No. The *big* guy. He sat in that chair over by the history section."

"Nope. Ms. Scott frowns on homeless inside the library. I would have remembered. Must have been when I wasn't there."

"Must have been," Abigail said. She hung up and turned to Tony.

"He doesn't exist," Tony said.

"Not in *this* world."

They walked back to their car in silence, and got in. Tony started the engine.

"Entertaining angels unawares," Abigail said. "Wow."

"Yeah. *Wow.*" There was something to her story. There was no way that dog could have dragged him out. Not a full grown man.

"Let's go home," Abigail said. She reached over and took Tony's hand. "We need to get ready to go over to your grandma's house."

Tony pulled out and they drove home in a contemplative silence.

Chapter Twelve

Abigail put on the new black dress she had bought for the Christmas Eve service at the church, and added the little gold Christmas ornament earrings that used to belong to her aunt. The plan was to go to Tony's grandma's house for dinner, then they would go to church together. Abigail wondered if Benny and his family would be there. She'd ask them how Lily was doing.

She came down stairs and found Tony already dressed, wearing a dark suit with a Christmas tie.

He whistled when he saw her. "A Christmas angel descendeth," he said. His eyes were twinkling, and she paused on the stairway for a moment just to take in the sight of him. She had almost lost him. And an angel had saved him. The thought of both made her heart ache, and she ran the rest of the way down the stairs and flung her arms around him.

"I like this!" Tony said, hugging her back. She felt his strong arms around her and held him close.

She could smell the pine from the Christmas tree. Tony had the local radio station on, and there was an advertisement playing for Christmas brunch at a restaurant in town. Cocoa came over, jealous, and started rubbing against Abigail's ankles, purring and demanding attention. Tony held Abigail close and put his lips close to her ear.

"*My bounty is as boundless as the sea, My love as deep,*" he whispered, "*the more I give to thee, The more I have, for both are infinite.*"

She loved it when he quoted Shakespeare to her. She briefly said a prayer of thanks to God for bringing this amazing, romantic, sexy man into her life. He *was* her life. He was her best friend. From where she was standing, she could see the angel wings ornament on their Christmas tree.

She turned her face up to him.

"'Romeo and Juliet'. My point."

He smiled, putting his forehead against hers.

"You know where we are?" he said.

"In our living room?" Cocoa pushed against Abigail's leg, more insistent for attention.

"Underneath the mistletoe," Tony said.

"Ohhhhhh, I like that," Abigail said, and pressed her lips against his. She felt him pull her close, and she silently sent a thank you up to Mr. Bates in Heaven. As they kissed, a song came on the radio:

Long ago on Christmas Eve,
The first there ever was,
An angelic host announced a birth,
Sent down from Love above...

The End!

Turn the page to learn how Tony and Abigail
first met!

Mrs. Chartwell
and the
Cat Burglar

Chapter One

Mrs. Abigail Chartwell filed away the last document in her stack and prepared to go home for the evening, but the gentleman at the counter kept *talking*. He was going on about some university course and how he was using certain historical documents to support his thesis, but she had stopped listening closely a while ago so she could leave the library before the weather got worse. There was a terrible snowstorm on its way. She checked the time on her phone.

"I need to leave now," she said, pushing her glasses up on the bridge of her nose and finally turning her full attention to the young man, who got flustered at the eye contact and choked on his words.

"Um…yes, of course. I'm sorry to have taken so much of your time." With flushed cheeks and ears quickly turning red, he exited the room, cutting through the Women's History section on his way out.

Abigail sighed. She was a beautiful woman, and most men couldn't meet her eyes for more than a few seconds before becoming tongue-tied. But she wasn't interested in flirting. She had experienced a brief marriage at the age of twenty-four, but her husband had died within months of their honeymoon, long before she had time to figure out how to navigate it. And that was some six long years ago.

She enjoyed her work at the library in the Ancient Maps and Documents department, and kept her thick red hair in a bun and her wide, beautiful eyes hidden behind glasses so as to discourage any interested potential courtiers.

Love wasn't even on her radar. Been there, done that.

Satisfied that her work area was tidy, she slipped out behind the Geography section, through Ancient Artifacts, and back to the break room to grab her coat. On her way, she set the alarms that secured the windows and central corridors, since it was her turn to close. She was the last to leave on Tuesdays. The collections of old books, maps and journals that the University's library housed were rare, and most were worth a fortune.

"Good night, Mrs. Chartwell," said the library's janitor, who had just pulled his bucket out of the closet. Bob had the security codes and could release them room by room as he worked.

"Good night, Bob," she said, waving her hand, which still bore her wedding ring. She made sure the light caught it. Bob had recently made some indirect moves that led her to believe he was taking an interest in her. She didn't have time for that.

Then she realized she was missing her gloves. She had pulled them on after lunch because it was cold in the stacks today and her hands were freezing. She had worn them all afternoon, so they must be back at her desk.

Bob disappeared on the elevator down to the basement. He always started at the bottom and worked his way up. Her department was on the second floor of the five-story building, and her desk was under a tall, domed skylight that let in the sunshine during the summer and an unpleasant draft during the winter.

She made her way back to her desk. There they were, on the floor under her chair. She bent down to pick the gloves up and noticed someone had knocked the Old Maps brochures off the desk at some point during the day and not bothered to pick them up. They lay scattered under the desk, out of reach. She got down on her knees, stretching her arm out as she tried to reach them. She had to crane her head to the side to get her arm that far under, but she managed to grasp most of them. She made another attempt, and when she had them all, she stacked them in a pile and stood up.

That's when she saw him.

He was dressed in black—some sort of tight outfit that looked like something a runner would wear. It covered his entire body, including his face, she noticed with a bit of fright. Only his eyes were showing.

He froze when he saw her. There was a long black rope hanging just above his head, threading its way up the three floors to the dome above them.

Abigail was about to scream when the man put his finger to his lips. Something about his movement stopped her.

"Good evening, ma'am," he said, and gave her a sweeping bow. "Welcome to the maps department."

That irked her. It was *her* maps department. And he was in it.

"If you move, I'll scream," she said, unsure as to why she hadn't already done so. Absurdly, she noticed he had amazing eyes. Dark brown. They twinkled as they gazed into hers.

"No reason to scream," he said. His voice was low, musical. "I'm not here to hurt you. I just wanted to check something out. Of the library." He pulled his hooded mask off, revealing thick, wavy black hair. "I'm Tony. Tony Russo. Pleased to meet you."

She reached behind her and pushed a button. It was a silent alarm they installed last year when they moved the classic maps in from France. She never thought she'd have to use it.

*Please God…*she prayed, not really sure how to finish the prayer.

He took a few steps closer to her.

If she could keep him talking, the police would be here soon. She wondered where Bob was.

"Russo? As in the famous painter?" She needed to kill time.

"Yes," he said, peering at her from under thick lashes. "I'm related."

"I don't believe you."

Antonio Russo was one of the world's most well known impressionists, with his works hanging in museums around the world, including the Louvre.

"Pity." He watched her calmly. "I just need one thing and then I'll leave."

She eyed the tube he was carrying. "You can come back during the day and check it out like a normal person. Instead of stealing it."

"You can't check this out."

He was right. The maps and documents in her department had to remain in the library.

"I'm here to *borrow* something. There's a difference. I plan to put it back."

Her eyes narrowed. "Is this a robbery?"

"This is most certainly *not* a robbery," he said, holding both hands up. "Robbers are armed. Thieves are not."

"I thought you said you weren't here to steal anything," she said. His lips twitched, as if he were about to laugh. Was he making fun of her? Her eyes traveled back to his and then to his hands, which were covered in black gloves. His skin-tight clothes, she noticed, outlined his body quite well. His *entire* body.

He took a few more steps toward her, and there was no longer a desk between them. The curls of his wavy black hair ended just above the nape of his neck. It was the type of hair you wanted to run your hands through.

She stared back at him. She felt her heart pounding in her chest.

"You won't get away with this," she said. "You're on camera."

"I disabled the cameras," he whispered. He was close enough now that she could smell his aftershave. Something a bit spicy. His breath was on her cheek and slightly minty. "And the security system. You usually leave promptly at 6 p.m. You're late tonight."

"So you *are* a thief."

"Maybe." He gently reached toward her cheek and behind her.

His hand slipped away from her face, and he held her hairpin between his fingers. She felt her hair fall down around her shoulders in a cascade of thick, soft, red waves. She smelled her lavender cream rinse and saw the thief swallow as his eyes traveled from her eyes to her hair. It was one of her best attributes, her hair. She had inherited it from her grandmother. Just like the pin.

"That's my grandmother's," she said, looking at the pin. "It's not worth anything."

Which was true. The jewels were fake, a 1940s costume jewelry piece. But it had sentimental value.

He looked at the pin in his hand and then back to her. He might be trying to charm her, but two could play at that game. She held his eyes.

"Did my heart love till now? Forswear it, sight! For I ne'er saw true beauty till this night," he whispered, his voice husky.

What? He was quoting Shakespeare at her? She held his gaze and frowned.

He seemed to gather himself. "At any rate, I've come to take what I need and I'll be going."

She wondered where the police were, or if he had also disabled the silent alarm system. She glanced at the clock. Bob was probably still in the basement.

"What are you looking for?" she asked, to keep him here. She wasn't about to let him get away with this…this…intrusion into her world.

He hesitated and then turned and walked a few steps away from her, twirling her hairpin between his fingers. His arms were strong, well muscled under his suit. "A map," he said. "There's an old Russo painting hidden in the city, and there's a map that leads there. I'm here to get that map."

"The portrait? That's a legend," she said. "It's not true. Treasure hunters would have found it years ago."

"But they don't have the information I have," he said. She noticed his cat-like steps as he paced around and how his body suit clung to him. He was in very good shape. Or maybe there was just a lot of spandex holding him together.

"What information?" She thought she heard sirens in the distance. But no, it was a silent alarm. They wouldn't put the sirens on.

"My great-great grandmother was rumored to have had an affair with Russo, and I am the descendant of that event. He couldn't marry her—because as you know from history, he was already married—but he painted a portrait of her and signed it with a heart next to his name. He called the painting 'Laurel,' after my great-grandmother. It was a nickname he had for her. Nobody knew who she was because back in that day to be pregnant out of wedlock was to be shamed."

"Nobody has ever proved that painting exists," Abigail said.

"Ahhh…but it does."

Abigail crossed her arms and sat down on her chair. "So you're telling me that you are related to Russo—the famous painter—by virtue of an affair and that you know where this world-famous painting is? The painting that every treasure hunter has been looking for for the past seventy years? The painting of the Mystery Woman?"

He turned to look at her. She had crossed her legs and taken off her glasses to chew on the frame, a nervous habit of hers. Her green eyes caught his dark ones. "Yes," he said simply.

She cleared her throat. "Well, go at it then. Go find your map."

He stood there, looking at her.

"What's your name?" he asked.

"Don't you know? I thought you had been stalking me."

"I don't know," he said. "I only watched to see who left the library and when. I don't *stalk*."

"Mrs. Chartwell," she said out of habit.

"Mrs.?"

She fingered her ring. "He died." She didn't usually share that information.

"Oh. I'm sorry."

"Yes."

"What's your first name?"

"That's none of your business."

"But I told you mine."

"Which was foolish. I'll use it to track you down once the police get here."

"The police aren't coming. I told you I disabled the alarms. We have time for some tea." He gave her a charming smile. She noticed he had a very nice mouth, with a shadow of a beard beginning.

They heard a crash as a door burst open somewhere.

"They're here," she said. "I have a secondary alarm, a silent alarm. I pushed it."

He swallowed hard and then met her eyes.

"You're beautiful."

She looked behind her. They'd be coming through that door.

"Go," she said, nodding toward his rope, suddenly wanting to keep him safe. "Go."

She turned her back to him, as the police burst through, guns out.

"Abby!" said the cop in the front. It was Jimmy Stout, an older policeman whom she knew. He had two others with him. He nodded to them, and they separated to right and left, guns ready.

"He's not armed," Abigail said.

"Who?" Jimmy asked.

"The thief," she said, turning back. "Don't shoot him."

But he was gone. There was nothing where he had been just a moment ago. She glanced at the dome and didn't see any sign of the rope. He had simply disappeared.

"Where is he?" Jimmy asked her. He followed her eyes overhead but she quickly looked down the stack, toward the Women's History section. She pointed. "He went that way. But he's gone."

"Clear," said one of the officers.

The other cleared his area and then they took to the stairs. "We'll cut him off below."

"Be careful," she shouted after them. "You'll scare Bob. He has no idea."

She could picture Bob mopping, humming along with his earbuds in.

"What happened?" Jimmy asked her. "Are you okay?"

"I'm fine," she said. "There was…there was a man. Here." She pointed to the floor in front of her. "I don't know where he went. He came to steal a map."

"A map?"

"That's what he said."

"Can you give me a description of him?"

She thought about it. His taut body leaning near hers, the dark eyes hidden under long lashes, the masculine mouth and strong hands. He was Italian, definitely, or of Italian descent. His hair was thick, like hers. And wavy. And his eyes were kind. Mischievous, but kind. He had meant her no harm.

"I didn't get a good look at him," she said. "He had a suit on. It was black. Like a cat burglar."

"And he wasn't armed?"

She pictured his tight suit, outlining…well, everything.

"No."

"You're sure?"

"Pretty sure."

"Did he steal what he came for?"

"I don't think so. You got here in time." There was no way he would have been able to get the map, which was locked up, and get out in seconds.

Jimmy's men came in then. "It's all clear. We don't see any sign of an intruder. Or of how he got in here. But somebody disabled the cameras and perimeter alarms."

Jimmy relaxed and holstered his gun. "Abby? You sure you're okay?"

Jimmy had been the cop who came to her house with the news the night her husband died. She had been alone, no family, and he had taken her to his home shortly after she collapsed, weeping. Jimmy's wife had made her hot tea and put a cold washcloth on her forehead and later made up the guest room bed for her. They were in their fifties with no kids of their own. Jimmy had checked on her regularly the first year, and his wife had made her meals for a while. After six years, Jimmy still stopped in to catch up with her, and she frequented their house for Sunday dinners.

"I'm okay," she said, but she was trembling.

"At least let us drive you home."

She nodded and closed her coat around her. Jimmy had to stay and finish up, but his younger partner drove her home and walked her up to the door. She was glad of the thick boots she wore, as the snow was quickly accumulating on the sidewalk.

"We'll catch him," he told her just before she went inside. "He won't bother you anymore."

"I don't think he's dangerous," she said. "I think he just wanted a map."

"Jimmy will call you tomorrow for some more details. You may have to come down to the station." He tipped his hat. "Good night, ma'am."

"Good night."

She turned the key in her ancient, three-story home on Blossom Street. She had inherited it from her aunt, and its many cozy rooms and twisty staircases appealed to the bookworm in her. Indeed, she had outfitted nearly every room with bookcases, which were mostly full.

She closed and locked the door, greeted her cat, and sat down to pull off her boots. She thunked the snow off them, shook the snow out of her hair, and tossed her glasses on the side table.

She went into her bedroom and opened her laptop, typing "Tony Russo" into a search engine. Nothing came up that looked like him. She looked under the White Pages. Nothing. She tried Anthony. Then she searched simply "Russo." About a hundred entries popped up under the name of the famous Italian painter. She scanned down and read an article about the "lost" painting.

Russo's "Mystery Woman" was rumored to be a portrait of his lover. Its whereabouts have never been discovered and historians and collectors wonder if it hangs in the home of Russo's illegitimate relatives or is hidden in the hands of a collector. Or, for that matter, if it even exists.

She closed her laptop and sat there, thinking about Tony. She hadn't been interested in a man since her husband and had never even thought about dating again. She was finished.

She touched her hair where his hand had lifted the hairpin out and closed her eyes, remembering his softly spicy cologne and those amazing eyes. She had felt something.

"It's ridiculous," she said to her cat. Cocoa, a petite tortoiseshell, rubbed up against her hand, wanting more attention and petting. "He's a thief. He doesn't even exist, according to the Internet."

Why was she protecting him? Why hadn't she been honest with Jimmy?

She ran her hand down the back of her hair, remembering his soft touch as he had quickly pulled the hairpin from it. And then the look in his eyes as he had watched her tresses fall. So he was enraptured by her beauty; most men were. So what? It didn't mean anything.

"I'm being stupid," she said, rubbing Cocoa behind the ears.

She went to fix herself a bowl of cereal for dinner. "After all, he's a thief." She thought she heard a window scrape open and went to check in the living room. It was only the wind outside blowing a branch against the house. The snow was falling harder now. It wasn't fit for man nor beast out there. She wondered if Tony had gotten home safe, wherever home was, or if Jimmy had found him. Surely they could track him in the snow.

She went to bed at 9:30, curled up in her big canopy bed under thick covers, but lay there long into the night thinking about the mysterious man who came to steal her map and quoted Shakespeare love lines. She finally fell asleep with a slight smile on her face.

To continue reading, pick up a copy of
Mrs. Chartwell and the Cat Burglar at
PamelaGossiaux.com, Amazon, or any book
store.

Other Books by Pamela Gossiaux

Meet Amy Summers, a big-hearted heroine whose simple life gets turned upside down when she finds a winning lottery ticket worth millions…but should she cash it?

Amy Summers has it all: the world's best job, an awesome boyfriend, and a happily-ever-after in sight. Then, in one very bad day that involves burnt toast and a police arrest, she loses everything – except for a winning lottery ticket her ex left behind.

Afraid to cash it, she decides to give up men and become a Bohemian novelist. She takes her laptop to Starbucks and literally bumps into caffeine-free, easy-going Josh Gray, a life coach and very handsome man. (Not that she's noticing.) When he offers to help Amy get back on her feet, she decides to hire him.

Her heart is telling her that he's the man for her, but Josh is big on honesty and Amy has a huge secret that could push him away if he ever finds out.

"Richly meaningful while wildly entertaining,
GOOD ENOUGH is a major new book by an exceptionally talented author."
– Grady Harp, Amazon Hall of Fame Top 100 Reviewer

"This story is such a fun read, it is impossible once you have opened it
not to be thoroughly captivated by Amy's escapades."
– Susan Keefe, *Midwest Book Review*

"GOOD ENOUGH touches a nerve every woman faces. Are we ever going to be good enough?
Gossiaux has written a funny, revenge romance that will have you cheering
on the heroine, Amy, until the very end."
—Diana Lesire Brandmeyer, author of CBA Best Seller *Mind of Her Own*

Available at PamelaGossiaux.com

About the Author

Pamela Gossiaux is the bestselling author of the *Russo Romantic Mystery* series, and the romantic comedy *Good Enough*, as well as the inspirational books, *Why Is There a Lemon in My Fruit Salad? How to Stay Sweet When Life Turns Sour*, and *A Kid at Heart*. Her YA book, *Ordinary Girl*, is an Amazon international bestseller, and proceeds from sales go towards helping the victims of human trafficking. Pamela is also a keynote speaker, writing instructor, and freelance writer. She lives and writes in Michigan near a wonderful university town with her husband, two sons, and three cats. Visit her website at PamelaGossiaux. com to learn more or to sign up for her newsletter.

www.ingramcontent.com/pod-product-compliance
Lightning Source LLC
Chambersburg PA
CBHW051926110726
47902CB00002B/433